"Get down!" Vicard barked, and Indy dropped face-first into the muck. An earsplitting cry from overhead sent an icy shiver down his spine. He forced himself to raise his head.

The sky was filled with a black form, and at first Indy couldn't imagine what it was. Then he saw massive, leathery wings and a prehistoric head that was all teeth and cold, dark eyes. The body of the creature was thick and snakelike, but with a pair of legs equipped with huge claws.

At first Indy couldn't make out what the creature was carrying. Then he looked on in horror as he realized the claws gripped the limp body of one of the guards.

"Was that the flying snake?" Indy managed to ask Salandra.

"Yes, a dragon," she answered. "And it's probably got a mate around here, too."

INDIANA JONES™
AND THE
INTERIOR WORLD

Rob MacGregor

BANTAM BOOKS

NEW YORK • TORONTO • LONDON • SYDNEY • AUCKLAND

INDIANA JONES AND THE INTERIOR WORLD
A Bantam Falcon Book / December 1992

FALCON and the portrayal of a boxed "ff" are trademarks of
Bantam Books, a division of Bantam Doubleday Dell Publishing
Group, Inc.

ISBN 0-553-29966-2

Published simultaneously in the United States and Canada

Bantam Books are published by Bantam Books, a division of Bantam
Doubleday Dell Publishing Group, Inc. Its trademark, consisting of
the words "Bantam Books" and the portrayal of a rooster, is
Registered in U.S. Patent and Trademark Office and in other
countries. Marca Registrada. Bantam Books, 666 Fifth Avenue, New
York, NY 10103.

PRINTED IN THE UNITED STATES OF AMERICA

RAD   0 9 8 7 6 5 4 3 2 1

To the folks on GEnie
who followed the adventure in the making.

The exterior world must inevitably be lined at every point with an interior one.

—Teilhard de Chardin

Whether it happened so or not I do not know; but if you think about it you can see that it is true.

—Black Elk

PROLOGUE

September 21, 1928
Channels of Paradise

Maleiwa and his two lieutenants moved rapidly through the channels. They were close to the passageway to the exterior and they knew it. But Maleiwa feared they would be late. The solar portal opened twice a year and only for a few minutes each time. They were anxious and paid no heed to anything behind them.

That was fine with Salandra. Maleiwa's intense concentration on finding the portal worked to her advantage. It allowed her to hurry after them with little concern about discovery. She was prepared to follow them wherever they went. It was up to her to keep track of Maleiwa's incursions into the exterior.

The Channels of Paradise, as this region was

known, was only vaguely mapped and seldom used because of the time limitations. But that made it ideal for the tall, muscular, bald-headed leader of the Wayua: He didn't want anyone to know about his secretive efforts to form an alliance on the exterior.

But he hadn't fooled Salandra. She'd been watching Maleiwa from a distance for a long time. She knew he wanted nothing more than to expand his base of power, and that attempt had to be stopped. The people of the exterior were not prepared to deal with him and what he represented. The lack of belief, more than anything, was their worst enemy. How could they confront what they did not believe?

There was a time when the ancient sorcerers from the outer world mixed freely with the denizens of the underworld. But those times were long past and lived only in the minds of a very few, and in the hearts of many legends. Now the younger brothers, as those on the outside were sometimes called, were particularly vulnerable. They had progressed in a way that led them to worship mechanical things. Machines had become their gods, and they had divorced themselves from the ancient knowledge. Maleiwa understood the vulnerability, and wanted to use it to his own advantage.

Salandra paused and hugged the wall as the men entered a round chamber. The room was dark and there was no sign of a passageway to the outside. Maybe they were too late, and had missed their chance. How satisfying it would be to report back to the king that Maleiwa had failed.

Suddenly, a harmonic ringing of chimes filled the chamber. The sound had no specific source but seemed to come from everywhere. The channels were inhabited by elemental beings, and their mellifluous music was their signature. It grew louder and louder and literally swirled around her. It momentarily disoriented her, but it didn't take long for her to understand what it meant.

Light flooded the chamber, pouring through a triangular-shaped portal that had appeared in the wall. Dawn had arrived in the outer world on the day known as the equinox.

She shaded her eyes, as did Maleiwa and his lieutenants. Even though they had prepared for the changes, the first exposure of intense light and the thickness of the outer air was nevertheless a shock. But there was little time to adjust. The portal was a temporary, fleeting opening. She had to prepare to rush out after Maleiwa, and still avoid detection.

She squinted against the brightness and saw Maleiwa climbing through the opening. His lieutenants had already gone ahead of him. Salandra rushed across the chamber as soon as Maleiwa was out of sight. The chimes resonating through her, the richness of sound filling her like water in a vessel. She didn't want to leave, but she knew she must. She had no choice; it was her duty, her mission.

She no sooner stretched a leg through the triangular opening in the rock wall when she saw movement in front of her and heard a jumble of voices. She quickly pulled back her leg, and pressed against the wall. Did Maleiwa suspect he was being followed? If so, she was caught. There was no time to escape. She would die right here, and no one would ever know what happened to her.

Maleiwa crawled back into the chamber. He was carrying something that looked like a sword or a staff.

It was milky white and the hilt was silver, shaped like a twin-headed bird, an eagle. What was it? What was he doing?

As Maleiwa raised the staff, the ground suddenly shuddered and a moment later, a deafening explosion tore through the chamber. Salandra was knocked to the ground. Maleiwa stumbled and fell to his knees, still clutching the staff. Dust and bits of rock filled the air. The portal closed; the light vanished. Maleiwa yelled for his lieutenants, but there was no answer. Salandra was confused, frightened. It wasn't supposed to happen that way.

Suddenly, the Wayua leader fled down the channel with the staff under his arm. She waited a moment, then raced after him at a safe distance. One thought was on her mind. She not only had to continue watching Maleiwa, but she had to find out everything she could about the staff.

1

RONGO-RONGO TABLETS

Spring 1929
Easter Island

The hand pick flashed in the waning light and stabbed the earth again and again. Finally, the soil was loosened, and Indy scooped it out with his trowel. Then he went to work with the hand pick once more. Over and over the same process repeated itself, as though it had nothing to do with him. This was the fifth house in the long-abandoned ceremonial village of Orongo, and the fifth time, it seemed, that he was coming up empty-handed. Tomorrow, he'd return and replace the dirt, and cover the floor with the same stones in the exact arrangement he'd found them, and move on to the next house.

The stone houses were situated precariously on the rim of Rano Kau. Most of them were still in good condition, even though seventy-five years had elapsed since the islanders had last climbed the volcano to praise the gods Makemake and Haua.

He raised the hand pick and struck again. He hit something solid. He dropped the pick, and carefully scraped the dirt aside with the trowel. A long, rounded wooden surface was emerging. At last. It looked like the edge of a Rongo-rongo tablet, the object of his search.

Although Easter Island was best known for its *moais*, the massive, solemn heads carved from stone, Indy's interest here was the wooden tablets, which were inscribed with a mysterious script. He'd been studying the tablets for weeks, but had gotten nowhere in his attempts to decipher the glyphs, which resembled stylized plants and animals. Supposedly, the islanders had forgotten how to read Rongo-rongo, and with only a few tablets in existence Indy had found the task of deciphering the system nearly impossible. So for the past couple of weeks he'd been digging in Orongo, hoping to uncover tablets that might provide the key to comprehending the script.

He set the trowel aside, picked up a brush with stiff bristles, and continued removing dirt. He'd been concentrating on the script so intensely that every night in his dreams the tiny creatures danced across his vision in sets of parallel lines. They motioned to him with their fins and fronds, arms and legs, stems and bills. They were telling him the key. Over and over again. It was so obvious. But only while he was asleep. Once he awoke, the images vanished and nothing was obvious.

Indy paused a moment and glanced over his shoulder toward the setting sun. He should stop now, and continue the work tomorrow. The sun would sink into the lapis waters in a matter of minutes, and he didn't like the idea of riding his horse down the slope of the volcano in the inky darkness. But it was no time to be practical, not after so many days of frustration. He needed to discover something for his own peace of mind. He couldn't go back to the States having accomplished nothing. Not that he hadn't been warned. Rongo-rongo script had been studied by linguists for decades and no one had cracked it.

He set the brush aside and began working with his fingers. He rubbed the dirt from the wood and leaned close. It was in good condition and wasn't about to crumble. Then he touched metal, and felt an acute sense of disappointment. It wasn't a tablet. But maybe it was a spear from the days of Captain Cook. He quickly worked his way along the metal. To his surprise it didn't taper to a point; it grew wider. He scraped furiously at the dirt, then abruptly stopped.

"Oh, no!"

He grabbed the wooden handle and jerked it free. *Ah, for crying out loud.* The only thing worse than finding nothing was digging up a blasted shovel.

He threw it to the ground in disgust. Another day of disappointment. He brushed the dirt off his hands, then gathered his tools in his pack. He slung it over his shoulder, and headed toward the far end of the village where his horse was tethered.

"Time to go, fella." Indy patted the horse's rear and was about to mount the steed when he glimpsed something moving in the rocks above his head. "Wait right here, Champ."

He climbed a narrow crevice between two boulders. Cautiously, he raised his head and looked

around, then smiled as several terns darted out from a
rocky recess. "What are you guys doing up here?"

Birds were special, even sacred, in Orongo, or at
least they had been at one time. In fact, the rocks on
which he stood were inscribed with drawings of creatures that were half men, half birds with long beaks,
each of them clutching an egg. The petroglyphs had
been carved by the followers of the birdman cult,
which had thrived for several centuries on the island.
Supposedly, the cult had died in 1862 when the island's king and many of his priests were kidnapped
and taken to Peru as slaves, thus ending the popu-
lace's knowledge of its ancient past.

Indy peered over the rocks and down into the lake,
which filled the crater of the dead volcano. A steam-
like fog was forming over the water, and the round
depression reminded him of a huge witch's cauldron,
or the home of a god. He raised his gaze and looked
out over the island. It was hilly and roughly triangular-shaped with a volcano at each corner. Much of the
land consisted of rough lava fields, which looked
nearly black now in the dying light. In contrast, the
slopes of the volcanos were gentle and grassy, and
still bathed in sunlight.

Indy climbed back down the rocks and walked over
to the horse. The south face of Rano Kau dropped
sharply, and beyond the cliffs were three tiny islands.
The largest, Motu Nui, was the nesting ground for
thousands of sea birds, and along with Orongo had
been the focal point of the birdman cult. Indy had
asked if any survivors of the cult still remained, figur-
ing they might know something about the Rongo-
rongo script. But so far he'd gotten only blank stares
and a few laughs from the islanders.

"Let's go, boy." He swung his leg over the horse's back. But he never reached the saddle. A figure dashed from the rocks, grabbed his pack, and jerked him to the ground.

A knife glinted in a ray of sunlight, and Indy rolled over just as the blade stabbed the dirt next to his throat. The man pulled it loose and stabbed again. This time, Indy grabbed his forearm, and they twisted and turned like dancers, edging closer and closer to the cliff.

Indy glimpsed the man's face and saw fear. He was just a kid, sixteen or so. He was slighter than Indy and no match for his strength. The knife dropped to the ground, and the kid tottered near the brink. A slight shove and he'd fall to his death, but Indy pulled him away. He grasped the boy's shoulders and lifted him up so his toes just touched the ground.

"All right, what's this about? Who are you?"

The kid shook his head, and gasped for breath. His eyes darted back and forth as if he were looking for a way to escape. Indy lowered him to the ground and loosened his grip. A mistake. With a powerful thrust, the kid kneed Indy between the legs, slipped out of Indy's grasp, and raced over to the archaeologist's horse.

"Oh, no, you don't!" Indy was doubled over in pain, but he managed to reach into his pack and jerk out his whip. He'd brought it along for diversion. It was good luck, part of his gear, and a weapon in a pinch.

He snapped it toward the kid just as the horse and rider galloped off. The whip fell harmlessly to the ground amid a cloud of dust. "I must be getting rusty."

As he reeled in the whip, he spotted the knife. He picked it up and turned it over in his hands. "Well, well. What do you know?"

The handle was wooden, and carved on it was a half-man, half-bird figure grasping an egg. Maybe the birdman cult was still alive, after all.

2

FALLEN MOAI

"Indy, where have you been? You almost missed supper."

"Evening, Marcus." Indy ambled across the restaurant and sat at the table where Marcus Brody and a few of the others on the expedition were eating. "I got delayed on the volcano."

A kid approached Indy, and for a moment he thought it was the same one who'd attacked him. He held a wooden figure up in front of Indy. It had a human face with a large, hooked nose, sharp cheekbones, and hollow cheeks. Its earlobes were long and complemented by a goatee. Its ribs and spine protruded and its hands and penis hung down to its knees.

"You want to buy, mister?"

Indy looked past the hand-carved demon, known as a *moai kavakava,* and saw it wasn't the same kid. "No, thanks. I've already got one."

"Just go on. Let us eat in peace," said an archaeologist named Howard Maxwell. "Obnoxious kids."

"They can be that way," Indy commented.

"So any luck up there, Jones?" asked Maxwell, a chunky, pug-nosed man with slicked-down hair that was always neatly parted in the middle. "We're leaving next week, you know."

"You don't have to tell him that, Howard," Brody said. "You can be as annoying as those young salesmen."

"It's all right, Marcus," Indy said. Brody was an Englishman who had lived in the States for years and was an old family friend and virtually a substitute father for Indy. "In fact, I did find something this afternoon."

"Oh, what is it?" Brody asked, his curiosity piqued.

A waitress brought Indy a glass of Chilean wine, and he took a sip. "A shovel. It was buried three feet under one of the floors."

Brody looked perplexed. "Well, I guess that means someone else has already been digging."

The others laughed. "The kiss of death," Maxwell crowed, making no attempt to hide his glee. He was a few years Indy's senior, and Indy sensed that the man had resented him from the first day, when Brody introduced Indy as one of the best young archaeologists in the field and classroom.

Indy decided not to say a word about the incident with the kid. He'd probably tell Brody about it later. Not only did he want to avoid sounding boastful or overdramatic, but he also wanted to see if any of the islanders who were helping them acted any differently toward him.

After he'd recovered enough to walk, he'd started

down the road, convinced that he would have to hike back to Hanga Roa, where the expedition was head-quartered. It wasn't far away as the crow flies, but the road down the volcano twisted and turned and seemed to go on forever. Then, half a mile from Orongo, he found his horse. From the footprints he was able to tell that the boy who had attacked him had switched horses, riding off on his own steed.

"I wonder if the shovel came from the east or the west," one of the others said.

"Oh, bother," Brody said. "Here we go again."

There was an ongoing discussion among the expedition members about whether the people who settled the island had come from the west, Polynesia, or the east, South America. Most were certain the islanders had arrived from other Polynesian islands. But Maxwell contended that the enormous *moais* that dotted the island's coastal area were built by the same South American Indians who had constructed massive stone cities on the mainland.

"Jones, what do you think?" Maxwell asked. "We have yet to hear your ideas on this matter."

Indy shrugged. "You guys are limiting the possibilities. I've heard theories that the original inhabitants were Egyptians, Greek Hindustanis, and even red-haired Caucasians from North Africa. They've even been called survivors of a lost continent."

"Good points, Indy," Brody said.

"Don't confuse the matter, Jones," Maxwell blurted. "Get serious."

"Okay, I think you're both right. Look at the legends. They talk of two groups arriving on the island, the Long Ears and the Short Ears. King Hotu Matua

and his followers came from the east, and Chief Tu-
ko-ihu and his people arrived from the west."

Maxwell waved a hand at Indy. "You can't count on
those old stories. They get all twisted around. You've
got to look at the facts."

"Where're your facts, Maxwell? Tell me that," demanded a Frenchman named Beaudroux.

"I've told you over and over. There are Peruvian
Indians who elongate their ears. They were the same
Long Ears who carved the *moais*."

Beaudroux, a tall, slender man, peered down his
long nose at Maxwell. "But do they live near the sea?
No. Do they make ocean-going vessels? Of course
not."

"The Indians who lived two thousand years ago
probably had an entirely different perception than
you do of an ocean-going vessel," Maxwell countered.

And so it went on and on. Indy's dinner, a lamb
stew, arrived as the discussion continued.

In spite of his difficulties with the tablets, Indy was
glad that he was working on his own, rather than ex-
cavating *ahus*, the stone platforms on which the *moais*
had been erected. That was the task which occupied
the others, except for Brody, who was constantly involved in mediations with the island's mayor to make
sure that everything went smoothly and to assure the
islanders that the visitors' intent was to obtain knowledge, not artifacts. But Brody had been bewildered to
find that the islanders wanted to sell him artifacts,
most of which were replicas of recent origin, like the
moai kavakava the boy was selling.

"Maybe Indy's right," Brody said when the com-
ments started to turn caustic. "There may be no one
simple answer. It's like the name of the island. Some

call it Easter Island, others call it Isla Pascua. The islanders call it Rapa Nui, and even *Te Pito o Te Henua*, the Navel of the World."

"We also call it *Mata Ki Te Rangi*, which means Eyes that Look to the Sky."

They all looked up to see an attractive, dark-haired woman. "That's a lovely name," Brody said. "Davina, I don't think you've met Indy yet. He's working up on Orongo."

Indy shook her hand. Davina had distinctive Polynesian features with deeply tanned skin and long, braided hair. She could have been thirty or forty. He couldn't tell. Her dark eyes met his for a moment. Her hand was cool, and her grip was firm.

"Davina is studying for a graduate degree at the University of Santiago. She's the curator of the local museum."

"Right," Indy said. "The one who's been away."

"I just returned from the mainland yesterday."

"Well, please sit down and join us," Brody said, pulling out a chair.

"No, thank you. I just wanted to say that the mayor has found several men who will help you raise the *moai*."

"Do they know how to do it?" Brody asked.

She nodded and smiled. "They have a method."

The mayor had allowed Brody to bring the team of archaeologists here to excavate as long as they re-erected at least one of the many fallen *moais*. Brody had quickly agreed, without thinking how they were going to raise a twenty-ton block of stone with no modern equipment. When no one came up with an answer, Brody had put off the task. When the mayor had finally inquired about what was taking them so

long, Brody had confessed his problem and asked the
mayor for suggestions.

"Well, that's a relief. When can they begin?"

"First thing in the morning," she said.

"We'll be ready."

"Good." She glanced at Indy again. "Nice to meet
you, Professor Jones."

"It's Indy. And speaking of names, why did they
call the island 'Eyes that Look to the Sky'?"

"Because of the *moais*. They once had large eyes
that gazed out to the heavens." She turned and
walked off.

"Indy, you will join us tomorrow, won't you?"
Brody asked. "I'm sure we can use your help."

"Be glad to." But Indy's thoughts were still on
Davina. She had been wearing a necklace, a silver
pendant shaped like a creature that was half man, half
bird, and grasping an egg.

According to the island's oral history, the Short Ears
had rebelled against the Long Ears who ruled the
island. During the civil war, many of the *moais* had
been toppled, and nowhere was the destruction of the
stone monuments more visible than the southern
coast.

Indy had counted at least a dozen fallen heads en
route to their destination, the *moai* which would be
re-erected. The procession of wagons and horseback
riders was led by the mayor, who proudly drove a
shiny black Model T. It was the only automobile on
the island, and he had named the vehicle Calvin.
Brody rode in front with the mayor, while Indy, Maxwell, and Beaudroux were seated in the rear. "At first,
I only drove Calvin for ceremonial purposes," the

mayor said, fondly patting the dashboard. "But now I drive him around all the time."

"Why do you call it Calvin?" Brody asked.

"I named it after your president, Calvin Coolidge." The mayor beamed.

"I haven't seen many filling stations on the island," Beaudroux remarked.

"There are none. I purchase gas by the barrel from supply ships."

"What a silly thing to say," Maxwell muttered. "Of course there are no filling stations."

"I'll grant that you're an expert on silliness," Beaudroux chided.

Indy, seated between the two men, couldn't wait until they reached their destination. His wish was soon granted as they motored around a curve and came to a stop in front of an *ahu* on which rested yet another fallen *moai.*

"Here we are. This is the one," the mayor said.

As soon as he was out of the Model T, Indy walked over to the monument. He wasn't sure how the mayor had selected the *moai,* but it hadn't been on the basis of its size. It was neither the smallest nor the largest of the toppled heads he'd seen.

About twenty islanders piled out of the wagons and dismounted from the horses. Indy looked around for Davina. He was carrying the ornamental knife he'd taken from the kid at Orongo, and was curious to see her reaction when he showed it to her.

"Well, what do you think, Indy?" Brody asked as he and Indy climbed atop of the *ahu.*

The *moai* was about twenty-five feet long, and its ear alone was as tall as Indy. "It'll be interesting to see how they think it should be raised. Maybe they'll just wake it up, and it'll sit up on its own."

Brody chuckled. "Wouldn't that be something. It would go along with the legend." According to the traditional story, the *moai*s had walked from the quarry to their stone platforms under the guidance of powerful priests.

Indy took a closer look at the platform on which the *moai* rested. "Has this *ahu* been excavated?"

Brody nodded. "An English expedition a decade ago. In fact, there are some bones and stone figurines in the museum that came from here." He paused, then added: "Let's hope the gods aren't angry about that."

Indy laughed. "Sometimes, Marcus, I actually think you might believe in spirits and gods."

Brody smiled. "Let's get to work."

The islanders were busy picking up stones and placing them in piles on either side of the *moai*. Meanwhile, several men approached the *moai* with long poles and worked them underneath the gigantic head. The poles bent into bows as several others pulled and climbed onto them. Indy thought that the poles would snap at any moment, but the men persisted. Others, who had mounted the *ahu*, dropped onto their stomachs, and pushed handfuls of pebbles underneath it.

So that was the way. It would probably take days, but the method just might work, Indy thought. He noticed that a surprising number of stones cluttered the area around the *ahu*, and now he wondered if they'd been brought here centuries ago to erect the *moai*.

Davina rode up on a horse, dismounted, and

walked over to the *ahu*. Indy didn't waste any time moving over next to her. "It's not exactly magic, is it?"

"Maybe this isn't the way it was done in the old days," she remarked.

"You mean, the good old days?" Indy asked with a laugh.

"In the case of Rapa Nui, the old days *were* indeed better than what has followed. The last hundred years have been a terrible time for us. We have lost everything, even our history. This island is no longer the center of the world; it is the end of the world."

Her fervor surprised him; she didn't seem the type to display passion about anything. "Then why are you here?"

She picked up pebbles and piled them on the *ahu*. "It is my home, and I want to protect our past."

"I thought you said the past was lost."

Davina pushed her dark hair away from her face. "Not everything is lost, but some people would like to steal what is left."

"Is that what you think I'm doing here?"

She bent down to pick up more stones. "I'm not sure about you. Not yet."

Indy pulled the birdman knife from a pocket in his pack and held it in front of her. "Take a look. I think you'll find this of interest. The design matches your necklace."

She stared at the knife, transfixed. She reached for it, then backed away from the *ahu* as she turned it over in her hands. "Where did you get this from?"

Indy was about to tell her what had happened on the volcano, but something in her reaction changed his mind. "I found it at Orongo."

"This belongs to my son, Manuel. I haven't seen

him for six months, and now I'm home and no one seems to know where he is." She backed away, still looking at the knife. "I have to go."

She ran over to her horse, leaped onto its back, and galloped away.

Nearly an hour later, the mayor called for a break. Indy stepped back from the *ahu* and was surprised to see that the top of the *moai*'s head had already risen several inches.

"Isn't it just amazing, Indy?" Brody said. "This must be the way they did it."

"Yeah, maybe." He pointed to the round topknot which lay several yards away. "But how did they put the hat on? They must weigh a couple of tons."

Brody touched a finger to his chin. "Now that's a good question. Let's see what the mayor has to say about that."

As they walked over to him, Brody cleared his throat. "Listen, Indy, I hope you haven't forgotten about Chiloé. I am still planning to go there as soon as we leave, and I really do hope that you'll—"

"Don't worry, Marcus. I told you I'd go with you. What did you say your friend's name was again?"

"Beitelheimer. Hans Beitelheimer. I just wanted to make sure everything was still all right."

"What do you think, gentlemen?" The mayor stroked his thick handlebar mustache.

"Impressive," Indy said.

"Yes, indeed," Brody put in. "But what about the topknot?"

"Don't worry about it. We're just going to leave that for now," the mayor said. "But it was probably lifted the same way, with little stones."

That would take a lot of stones, Indy thought, but he didn't say anything more. He spotted Davina returning on horseback. As she dismounted, he excused himself and headed over to her. "Any news about your son?" he asked.

She nodded. "Everything is okay. Now I understand. Manuel was afraid to talk to me, because of what happened. Thank you for not hurting him."

"Why did he attack me?"

"I can't explain now. Can you meet me at Anakena Beach this evening?"

"What do you have in mind?"

"The Matuans want to talk to you."

"Who are the Matuans?"

"A secret society which carries on the old ways."

Indy did his best to hide his excitement, but he knew he was about to make a breakthrough. "I thought the old ways were forgotten."

"What is known is kept secret so it can never be stolen again."

"What do they want with me?"

"You've proven yourself, and they want to talk about the Rongo-rongo tablets."

"I'll be there."

"Come alone, and tell no one."

3

THE MATUANS

The water glistened under the stars as Indy walked along the beach toward the distant glow of a camp fire. Anakena was the largest beach on the island and the legendary place where Hotu Matua landed fifteen hundred years ago. Now, it might also turn out to be the beach where the puzzle of the Rongo-rongo script was finally solved.

Indy wasn't sure what awaited him. It could be trouble. But the risk was worth it. He hadn't told Brody what he was doing; Marcus would surely think it was too dangerous. He wouldn't stop Indy, but he'd worry. By now, Brody would be tucked in bed with a book, which was probably the best place for him.

As he moved closer to the fire, he saw several silhouettes gathered around it. Suddenly, a bird darted low overhead and cried out as if to announce his arrival. Indy glanced after the bird, then nervously tugged at his fedora, and touched his coiled whip.

One of the men said something as he entered the glow of the blaze. Suddenly, several people moved away from the fire and drifted off into the darkness. *Swell. What's going on?*

"Hello, Indy."

He spun around. "Davina! Where did you come from?"

She smiled. "Relax. No one's going to harm you."

She wasn't exactly convincing. "Where did everyone go?"

"They're on the way to the cave."

Indy knew that the lava-covered island was pocketed with caves. Some of them had once been inhabited, and others had probably been used for ceremonial purposes. He'd inspected a couple of them, and had been told that earlier expeditions and many islanders had dug in the caves looking for artifacts. So he'd figured Orongo, which was thought to be inhabited by ghosts, was a better place to dig for the tablets.

A bearded man with dark eyes emerged from the darkness. Firelight flickered across his face, making his features appear to shift from one moment to the next.

"This is Raoul," Davina said. "He's the one who opened the door for you."

"Are you the one who told Davina's son to stick me with a knife?"

"Manuel is also my son," Raoul said. "He was being tested, as were you."

"I think you were playing a dangerous game with your son," Indy snapped.

"Neither of you was meant to die. So neither of you did. Now why do you want to read our tablets?"

Nothing like getting right to the point. "To learn from them. To preserve the knowledge."

"That is the job of the Matuans. Not yours."

"But why must you keep it a secret?"

"There has been good reason. You know our history. But maybe it is time for us to change our ways. Makemake has told us in dreams that a worthy outsider must be given the opportunity to learn *ko hau motu mo rongorongo*."

"That means 'lines of script for recitation,' " Davina said.

Raoul nodded. "We think you are that person." With that, he walked off into the darkness away from the sea. Indy glanced at Davina and she pointed after Raoul.

Indy sensed that Raoul was telling him the truth. He felt like a man who had just stumbled upon a treasure chest filled with gold. He just hoped it wasn't fool's gold.

They walked for half an hour into the hills, before they stopped near an outcropping of rock shrouded by underbrush. Now Raoul seemed uneasy. He stared past Indy into the darkness. "Did someone follow you?"

"I came alone just like I was told. Trust me."

"I feel we are being watched from a distance. How did you get here?"

"By horseback. I walked the last few hundred meters."

Raoul smiled and seemed more at ease. "It's your horse. He's wondering what happened to you."

"They call that horse sense," Indy said.

Raoul pushed aside the thicket and motioned for them to enter. At first Indy saw nothing, then Davina disappeared into the darkness and he blindly plunged ahead. If they were lying to him, it was all over. One of the others he'd seen at the fire could club or stab or shoot him. Maybe they already had dug a grave inside the cave and just wanted him to get closer to it on his own. But he pushed aside his morbid thoughts as a match flared behind him, and Raoul lit a torch. They were inside a tunnel with just enough room to stand up.

"Stay close behind me," Raoul said. "Don't wander off."

"Wouldn't think of it," Indy said as they passed a channel branching off to the right, then another to the left. The tunnel forked again and Raoul headed down the arm on the right. Indy tried to pay close attention to every turn, memorizing the route.

A short distance later, light filtered from a room to one side of the corridor, and Indy knew they'd arrived. They entered a rectangular chamber that was more than thirty feet long and nearly half that wide. The roof rose at least twenty feet. They stopped near the center of the room and it took a moment before he saw the others sitting in near darkness along the wall.

"Manuel," Raoul said.

One of the seated figures immediately stood and moved toward them. Indy recognized the kid he'd fought at Orongo. He held something in both of his arms. It was covered with a colored cloth that bore the now familiar birdman design on it.

"Swell to see you again, kid." Indy's cynicism spiked his voice.

Manuel met his gaze. If he was afraid of Indy, he didn't show it.

Raoul pulled back the cloth, revealing a stack of inscribed tablets, six or seven, Indy figured, more than the total known to exist.

"Are they authentic?" he asked.

"Of course they are," Davina answered. "You will have plenty of time to examine them, but only in private and only with the Matuans present."

Indy reached toward the pile and felt Manuel's muscles tighten.

"It's okay," Davina said, then nodded to Indy. Carefully, he picked up the top one, and balanced the tablet on the palm of his hand. Davina held the torch over it, revealing an irregular, flat wooden board with rounded edges. The surface was covered with row after row of neatly engraved Rongo-rongo symbols, the same stylized plants and birds, four-legged creatures and odd figures that he had been studying.

"How many do you have?" he asked.

"Dozens. Maybe two hundred," Raoul said. "All well hidden."

"Two hundred?"

"It will take you months, even years of work just to catalog them," Davina said, "and even longer to comprehend what they mean. But we will help you."

Indy nodded, fighting an urge to laugh, to shout, to slap Raoul on the back. He couldn't believe his luck.

"There's just one thing," Raoul said.

Indy handed the tablet back to Manuel. He knew there had to be some catch. "What's that?"

"You can't begin your work yet."

"Why not?"

"We don't want the others you are here with to be involved. You will have to wait until they have gone."

"I see."

No problem there, Indy thought gleefully. That was only a few days away. He'd have to stay behind, of course, but with a discovery like this one, extending his leave shouldn't be any problem. That is, as long as his work was not a secret.

"I assume I can publish my findings when I'm finished, or even before."

"Of course," Davina said. "But you must be discreet about how you came upon the tablets. Most of them must remain hidden, but you can photograph all of them."

It was almost too good to be true. Then another thought occurred to him. "Why haven't you done this yourself?" he asked Davina. "You're in a perfect position. You're not only an islander, but you've been educated in the outside world."

She shook her head. "I am also a Matuan, like Raoul and Manuel," she explained. "The Rongorongo tablets are sacred to us. I could never use them for academic purposes." She glanced at her husband. "Yet, we understand it is time to make the world aware of who we are, and where we came from."

"And you will be surprised," Raoul said. "You can count on that."

"But what do you expect to gain?"

"Many people will come here when they find out about your discovery. Rapa Nui needs visitors, people who will come here on our terms and respect us while enjoying our island. There is great potential for our future. We are a poor people, and barely know how to accommodate visitors. But we will learn and prosper."

So that was it. It seemed like a long shot to Indy. But airplanes were getting larger and faster, and more

and more people would be flying them for pleasure.
Even though Easter Island was never going to be
around the corner from anywhere, it might someday
be reached in a few hours from the South American
mainland. "You might have something there."

"Then you'll extend your stay?" she asked.

"I need to talk with Marcus Brody. But I don't see
any big problem."

As he stepped outside again a few minutes later, he
took a deep breath. Incredible, he thought. Just incredible. He gazed up at the star-filled sky, and
smiled broadly. "Thank you, Makemake," he whispered.

The raising of the *moai* had won the hearts of the
islanders, and it seemed that everyone wanted to par-
ticipate. The work was continuing around the clock
with the mayor, Davina, Beaudroux, and Maxwell
putting in six-hour shifts to supervise the work crews.
The monument now stood at a sixty-degree incline,
and was rising several inches an hour as the islanders
continued working with pebbles and poles. Only two
days remained before the boat would leave with the
archaeologists for the mainland, but everyone agreed
that the monument would be standing upright before
they were gone.

Maxwell was in charge at the moment, and he was
dancing around, shouting orders and waving his
hands. At breakfast this morning, Maxwell had held
up a round stone, as if it were a talisman, and boasted
about the paper he would write describing his theory
on how the islanders moved and erected the *moais*.
He was certain that they had dragged the massive
carved stones on wooden planks, which had been

rolled over smooth round stones. Even though Indy had overheard the mayor explaining the same ideas to Maxwell, the archaeologist claimed it was his own theory. Beaudroux had responded that Maxwell could have the theory, because it was wrong. That, of course, had set off another argument.

"He's certainly in his glory," Indy said as he and Brody stood back from the crowded *ahu* and watched.

But Brody wasn't listening to Indy. "You mean to tell me that you saw hundreds of Rongo-rongo tablets and you didn't tell me about it?"

Indy shook his head. "I only saw a few of them, and I *am* telling you about it. They looked authentic from what I could see."

"I'm just flabbergasted. And they know how to read them?"

"So they say."

"Why aren't you in the cave now working with these Matunos?"

"Matuans," Indy corrected him. Then he explained the reason for the delay.

"Well, you've got to stay and see this thing through. I'm sure you won't have any problem getting a leave for the semester, or even a year. Why, you're on the verge of single-handedly cracking the mystery of Easter Island. You will end all the speculation about where the islanders came from, and why they created the *moais*." He glanced toward Maxwell, and added conspiratorially: "And even how they moved them."

Indy watched as one of the poles wedged under the *moai* snapped under the weight of several islanders. It was immediately replaced by another pole, and the islanders went right back to work. "Well, I figure that at the very least I should be able to crack the riddle of

the script. It may reveal the history of the island, and
it may not."

Brody had a mischievous glint in his eye. "Maxwell
is going to be so miffed when he finds out that you've
outdone him."

"I'm not worried about him, Marcus. But I was
concerned about our plans to go to Chiloé."

"Oh, dear." Brody touched a finger to his chin and
frowned. "It completely slipped my mind. This does
put something of a crimp in things. I was so hoping
you'd come to the island with me."

Indy gazed toward the *moai* as Maxwell frantically
waved for more men to hang on the poles. He hated
to disappoint Brody, but he didn't fully understand
why the museum director wanted Indy to accompany
him. "Tell me about this friend of yours. Who is he?"

"You mean I haven't told you that Hans Beitelheimer married the daughter of a dear friend of
mine from college days?"

"No, you haven't."

"Loraine was my goddaughter. She died several
years ago in a skiing accident," Brody explained. "She
met Hans at art school in Switzerland. They'd been
married six years when she was killed. Buried in a
landslide. They never found her body. Hans felt he
couldn't go on without her, but rather than take his
own life, he decided to go to the end of the world and
stay there. Chiloé is where he ended up."

Too bad Beitelheimer hadn't come here, Indy
thought. "And he's still on Chiloé?"

"Well, that's a good question. I've kept in touch
with him over the years. We usually exchanged a letter or two a year, and I've promised more than once
that I'd visit him. But then about two months ago, just

before we left New York, I received a most peculiar message from him. He sent me a telegram and said he needed my help."

"What kind of help?"

"That's the odd thing. He said that he was trapped in a legend, and didn't know if he could get out alive."

"What's that mean?"

Brody shrugged. "I don't know. But I thought you'd be interested in looking into it with me. I wrote him a note that I was about to leave for Easter Island, and that I'd visit him as soon as I could."

"I'll tell you what, Marcus. I'll talk to Davina and tell her I'm going to the mainland for a couple of weeks, and I'll be back as soon as I can."

Brody perked up. "Do you think that'll be all right with the Matuans? I don't want to cause any problems."

Indy shrugged. "They weren't in any particular hurry to show me the tablets. I've got the feeling it'll work out just fine."

"That's great, Indy. We'll find Hans in Chiloé and play it by ear from there. If it's really nothing much, you can leave in a few days, and head right back here. And I'll take care of all the details concerning your leave. You don't have to worry about a thing."

Indy grinned. "It's a deal."

4

Trapped in a Legend

June 1929
Isle of Chiloé

Summer in New England was winter at the bottom of South America. In Santiago, the temperature had been mild, but now they were more than five hundred miles to the south of Chile's capital and the weather definitely fit the country's name.

Indy zipped his leather jacket to the neck and tugged his fedora low over his eyes, a shield against the frigid breeze. The sun was hovering above the lapis sea, varnishing the surface with an orange glow as he and Brody walked onto the main pier of the town of Ancud.

Boats were docked two and three deep, and fishermen were busy unloading their catches. *Chiloé* literally meant 'land of sea gulls,' and hundreds of gulls swept across the sky, crying raucously, diving into the icy waters for discarded bits of fish.

Indy and Brody had spent a total of seventeen hours on the train from Santiago to Puerto Montt, the end of the line. From there, they'd ridden a carriage to the dock and ferried out to Chiloé. The island was about one hundred and seventy-five miles long and thirty-five miles wide. Its two main towns were Ancud and Castro, and there were numerous fishing villages. Potatoes and wheat were grown there, but much of the island remained thickly forested.

"Excuse me, sir," Brody said, interrupting a fisherman. "Do you know a man, an artist, named Hans Beitelheimer who lives here?"

The grizzled man looked up, studied Brody a moment, then shook his head.

"This is strange," Brody muttered as they moved on. "Beitelheimer has clearly been living here. I haven't been writing to a ghost, for God's sake, and he sent the telegram from here."

Their first stop had been the post office, but they'd found out that Beitelheimer's postal box didn't exist, and no one at the post office had ever heard of him. "And you said he's been writing letters to you?" Indy asked.

Brody stepped carefully around several salmons spread out on the pier. "Actually, come to think of it, there haven't been any letters from him for two or three years."

Indy glanced up at the careening gulls. "But you've been writing him all along?"

"Well, I sent him a card every Christmas. I guess I hadn't realized it had been so long since I'd heard from him. But then I got the telegram, as I said."

"Maybe you should've come here sooner."

"I thought of that. But you have to understand that Hans is a very dramatic man. He has a tendency to overstate things and overreact to situations."

Moving to Chiloé no doubt was a good example, Indy thought.

Brody peered into a pail and made a face. "What in the world . . . Do people eat those things?"

A fisherman on the nearby boat laughed and responded in heavily accented English. "Of course. You try one. You'll like it."

Before Brody could refuse, the man reached into the pail, picked out a spiny black sea urchin, and set it on the pier. With several swift and proficient slashes of his knife, he cut off the sharp spines, then sliced the creature in two, revealing a glistening, jellylike substance the color of a cantaloupe. The man then pulled a lime from his pocket, cut it open, squeezed it over the halves, then handed one half to Brody and the other to Indy.

Brody made a face. "What do I do with it?"

The fisherman made a motion with his hand. "Eat. There. Look at your friend."

Indy swallowed the sea urchin in two gulps. "Go ahead, Marcus. It's not bad."

Brody hesitated, then daintily tipped up the urchin shell as if he were drinking from a shot glass. He cleared his throat, touched his lips. "Yes, quite tasty, if I do say so."

"It looks like a good catch today," Indy commented to the fisherman.

The gray-haired man raised his weathered face. "Sometimes, the pier is piled with fish. Other times, not so many. We have a story here." He pointed out to sea. "We say that when we spot a mermaid in the morning, we can tell whether it will be a good day at sea or a bad one by the direction she is looking. If she is facing the shore, it will be a good day. If she looks out to sea, it won't be so good."

"Have you seen any mermaids?" Indy asked.

The man adjusted the rope that moored his boat to the pier. "I've seen many things around here. But I don't talk about them."

He turned away, but Brody called after him. "One moment. Do you know of a man named Hans Beitelheimer? He is a tall blond man, an artist. He paints pictures, I believe."

The fisherman stopped in the doorway of the rustic, wooden cabin on his boat. "I don't know that name, but there was a man who used to live here, a painter who looked as you said. He was foreign, and spoke with an accent."

"Do you know where we can find him?"

"He's gone now for maybe three years."

"Where did he go?" Indy asked.

The fisherman slowly shook his head.

"Who would know?" Indy asked.

"Talk to Jorge. He owns the Caleuche, a restaurant." He pointed up the hill toward the main street of Ancud. "He knew the man you are talking about. But he was called Juan. Juan Barrios, I think."

"That explains it," Indy said as they picked their way through a growing crowd of shoppers and fishermen on the pier. "He changed his name."

"It's possible," Brody answered. "At least we have a lead. We'll soon find out if this Juan and Hans are the same. The only thing that bothers me is that he isn't here any longer."

"Maybe he moved to another village," Indy said, wondering if Brody would mind if he left tomorrow for Santiago. There was a boat leaving for Easter Island in three days.

Brody smiled as they crossed the street and headed up the hill. "I hope so. I'm just a worrier. I can tell you're still thinking about Easter Island and all those Rongo-rongo tablets."

Indy shrugged. "The tablets aren't going anywhere, and Davina assured me that we could begin work as soon as I returned."

"It is an incredible opportunity," Brody said. "Ah, here we are."

A sign on the front of the restaurant pictured a sailing ship; beneath it was the name, *Caleuche*. They walked inside. A large table surrounded by eight or nine men was the only one occupied. They all turned and stared as Indy and Brody sat down. "I guess they're not used to strangers here," Brody muttered.

"Maybe not in the dead of winter." Indy looked up at a painting on the wall above their table. It depicted an old sailing ship like the one on the sign, but this one looked like a mirage, with the background visible through the ship. He was about to comment on it when a mustached man with a soiled white apron wrapped around his expansive girth approached them from the bar and greeted them.

"What do you suggest for dinner?" Brody asked. "I know it's early, but we've had a long journey from Santiago."

The waiter, who Indy hoped was also the owner, waved a hand. "It is no problem. I suggest our seafood platter. It is our specialty any time of the day."

"Sounds good to me," Indy said.

"And a bottle of your best white wine," Brody added.

"All of our wines in Chile are very good, but I will select a favorite of my own for you. You are English?"

"I hail from England, but I live in New York now. I'm a museum curator, and my friend here is an American, an archaeologist."

"Very interesting." The waiter pointed at Indy. "He digs into the past, and you put it on display."

"That's one way of looking at it," Brody responded. "Are you the owner?"

"Yes, I am. Allow me to introduce myself. I am Jorge Fernandez, at your service. Let me get your wine, and if you have any questions about Ancud or the island, I will do my best to help you."

"Congenial fellow," Indy said when Fernandez walked away.

"So it seems. I was hoping that by telling him about us he will be more willing to talk about Hans."

Indy pointed at the painting. "It's initialed J.B., as in Juan Barrios?"

"You're right."

Fernandez returned to the table, and poured two glasses of wine. "We were noticing this interesting painting here," Brody said in a casual voice after they had tasted and approved the wine. "Can you tell us anything about it?"

Fernandez laughed. "I can tell you all about it. That is the *Caleuche*. It is a ghost ship many people say they have seen."

"Why did you name your restaurant after it?" Brody asked.

"Because I too have seen it passing by the island late at night." Fernandez leaned over the table in such

a melodramatic manner that Indy suspected he'd put
on this performance many times for visitors. "It was
very brightly lit, and you could see the crew and hear
their strange music. It was so captivating that I had to
hold myself back. I wanted to run to the water and
swim to the ship, even though at the same time I was
very afraid."

"That's fascinating," Brody said. "But can you tell
me about the artist? What's his name?"

Fernandez's animated behavior abruptly ceased.
He stepped back. "He's not here any more."

"Did Juan Barrios paint that picture?" Indy asked
as the restaurant owner started to move away.

Fernandez's face was a road map of suspicion.
"How do you know his name?"

"I'm a friend . . . a relative of sorts," Brody said.
"What was his real name?"

Brody told him.

Fernandez nodded. "Very few people on Chiloé
knew him by that name. He changed it to fit in better."

"What happened to him?" Indy asked.

"Let me see about your dinners, and we will
talk."

"He knows something, doesn't he?" Indy said, as
the restaurant owner disappeared into the kitchen.

"I was about to say the same thing." Brody's eyes
moved across the restaurant as if he were searching
for more clues. "I always did love a mystery."

"And this one's complete with a ghost ship," Indy
said.

Their meals were identical, heaping plates of cobia
and lobster, clams and squid, potatoes and asparagus.
As they ate, Indy kept glancing at the painting of the

Caleuche. Something about it disturbed him. The crows, he thought. That was it. At least a dozen tiny crows were perched near the bow of the ship. What bothered him was that he hadn't noticed the birds at first. It was almost as if they'd appeared since he'd first set eyes on the ghost ship.

When they had finished eating, Fernandez returned to the table with a tall bottle filled with a golden liquid, and two glasses. "This is our specialty, made here in Ancud. *Líquido de oro.* Liquid gold. I think you will like it. Please, be my guests."

He poured a small amount in the glasses, and watched their reactions as Indy and Brody sipped. Indy had to admit it was delicious, and Brody agreed.

Fernandez beamed, then poured more into their glasses. Brody motioned to the empty chair. "Please, Mr. Fernandez, would you have a few minutes to sit down and join us?"

The restaurant owner glanced around, then nodded. "It's still early. I will be honored to join you."

As soon as he sat down, Fernandez began a monologue about the island, telling them about its various towns, his favorite restaurants, and the best food to order. He went on endlessly about seafood: the succulent clams and freshwater prawns, marine crabs with spotted shells, snails and giant mussels, and best of all, lobsters from the San Fernandez Islands. He patted his expansive stomach and suggested they try a corn pie called *pastel de choclo*, and also *humitas*, which were similar to Mexican tamales without all the spices, and of course, *empanadas*, a pastry turnover stuffed with chopped meat, fish, chicken, onions,

hard-boiled eggs, raisins and olives. When he turned
to the wines, Brody interrupted and asked if Barrios
had come here very often.

"Before he went away, yes. He would sit at this
very table under his painting. It was just one of many
that he made of the ship and other strange things
around here."

"What sort of strange things?" Indy asked.

Fernandez raised a finger, leaned forward, whisper-
ing: "You can't trust the birds."

"What do you mean?" Indy stole a glance at the
painting to make sure that the crows were still there.

"There are witches around here who can turn
themselves into birds."

Brody cleared his throat. "In the States, we call
stories like that old wives' tales."

"Please go on," Indy said, curious to hear what Fernandez had to say. "What's that got to do with Barrios?"

The front door opened, and several people hurried
in from the cold. "I have to go back to work now, but
if you want to talk about Barrios, come back here
when we close. I will take you to my house. I have
something to show you."

As it turned out, Fernandez meant exactly what he
said. It was close to midnight when he led them from
the restaurant to a two-bedroom cottage on a hill
above the town. He turned on a couple of gaslights
revealing walls covered with paintings. Every one of
them, Indy noted, was initialed J.B., and the subject
matter, without exception, was of a mystical nature.
There were lots of birds, some of which blended with
women flying on brooms. Traditional sorcery. There

were other paintings of people. Mysterious, menacing men dressed in black, alluring mermaids leaning against a rock in a harbor, and odd women with one side of their faces painted black.

"My God," Brody muttered. "That's him."

Brody pointed to a painting of a man with pale blond hair and skin so translucent that the veins on his nose were clearly visible. The wrinkles around his pale blue eyes suggested he was in his late fifties. But it was his expression that caught Indy's attention. He looked tortured.

Fernandez had opened a bottle of wine. He poured them each a glass, and they sat down at a wooden table in the dining room. "The people of this island are an industrious sort, but you will find that they are also wary of strangers. They have good reason."

"Witches?" Indy asked.

Fernandez nodded toward one of the paintings of the *Caleuche*. "Powerful ones. The ship's crew."

"Hold on, now." Brody looked baffled. "You're saying that the witches come from the ghost ship?"

"They've been terrorizing this island for hundreds of years. The people here are very careful not to hurt birds, because the legend says that if any harm comes to a crew member while he is transformed, the guilty one will either be killed, or abducted and condemned to sail the seas forever as a galley slave."

"Have you ever encountered any of them?" Indy asked.

"Maybe flying overhead in the shape of a crow, or as strangers like yourselves. But I've been fortunate. I've had no trouble with them, not like Juan Barrios."

"Now we're getting somewhere," Brody said.

Indy's gaze slid over to one of the paintings with

the menacing faces again. "Did he tell you that he's seen them?"

Fernandez drained his wine glass, and set it on the table. "One day I asked Juan to paint the ghost ship for my restaurant. I was not a believer in the *Caleuche* then. I thought the name would attract attention. That was all. To me the ghost ship was a legend, nothing more. But once Juan had painted the *Caleuche,* everything changed for him." Fernandez pointed at one of the paintings of faces. "They haunted his thoughts, and eventually visited him. Repeatedly."

"And he told you about it?" Brody asked.

"He didn't tell me everything. But one night he took me out to see the ship, and it was just as I told you earlier. That convinced me it was more than legend."

"But what happened to Hans . . . or Juan?" Brody asked. "Do you have any idea?"

Fernandez walked over to a window and spread the curtains apart. Bright moonlight streamed through the glass. He turned, facing them, his face in shadow. "Let me tell you another story. A few weeks ago, I was visiting an old man, named Marcelino, who had invited me to his house. There was another old fellow sitting in the corner, who didn't greet me, or say anything. He seemed so remote that after a while I just ignored him. Finally, Marcelino explained that the man was his brother, Teotoro, who had disappeared one night fifty years ago."

"Fifty?" Brody asked, incredulously.

Fernandez nodded. "Several weeks earlier Marcelino had been feeling nostalgic about Teotoro. Marcelino had been only eighteen when his brother vanished. He visited their old home on the banks of the Rio Pudeto, and there, seated in the living room and dressed as he'd been half a century earlier, was his brother. When Marcelino asked where he'd been all those years, Teotoro replied only that he'd been on a ship and implored him not to ask anything more."

"The ghost ship?" Brody asked.

Fernandez ignored the question and continued the story. "I went over to the man and asked him if he knew anything about Juan Barrios. He nodded and said that he was there on the ship. That was all he would say."

Brody looked disappointed. "That's it? You don't know anything else?"

"There is one other thing." Fernandez walked over to the table, poured more wine into his glass, and tipped the glass to his lips. "The last time I saw Juan he said something very strange to me. I didn't know what to think. He told me that he'd seen his wife, Loraine, on the ghost ship, and that he was going to join her."

"But it couldn't have been her," Brody protested. "No, she's dead."

Fernandez touched his temple. "They found her inside his head. If these evil beings can change to birds, they can look like anything they want. They created her to lure him aboard."

Indy had heard enough. "Could you take us to where you and Juan saw the *Caleuche*?"

"Right now?" Fernandez asked.

Brody jammed his hands in his pockets. "It's awfully late, Indy."

"I don't think you look for ghost ships at noon, Marcus."

"But, do you really think—"

"I'll take you there," Fernandez said. "But I can't guarantee your safety."

"Who said life ever came with guarantees," Indy snapped. "Let's go."

5

TWO BEITELHEIMERS

In the moonlight, the peninsula on the northwest corner of the island looked barren and uninhabited; the desolation of the place suffused Indy with a dark gloom that he couldn't shake. They'd taken Fernandez's carriage, riding west to the end of the dirt road. Then they'd hiked over a couple of rugged hillocks as they headed toward a prominence jutting toward the sea.

Indy picked at Fernandez's story as they walked, puzzling over every detail. He was still anxious to get back to Easter Island, but he was also curious about Beitelheimer and the ghost ship. He kept thinking about Beitelheimer's last message to Brody. *Trapped in a legend.* Indy still wasn't sure what that meant, but it was starting to make sense.

The landscape was steep and rugged, and the going was slow. Indy took his time, waiting for Brody and Fernandez, who were gasping for breath. Finally, he climbed the last few steps. Several feet in front of him, the land dropped precipitously. Beyond the abyss, ripples of silver moonlight glazed the dark sea. It wasn't hard to imagine a luminous ghost ship sailing through these waters.

"I don't remember it being such a climb," Fernandez puffed.

"I'll remember it that way," Brody said.

"This is where you stood?" Indy asked.

Fernandez nodded as he recovered from the hike. "Right here. We waited maybe one hour when we saw the ship rising from the sea."

"From beneath the water?" Brody asked.

"First I heard faint music." Fernandez spoke in a hushed voice as if he were afraid of being overheard. "It grew louder and louder, then the ship rose from the depths. It was all lit up, and before long I could see people on board. Men and women dancing, drinking. I don't know how to describe the music; it was music of the sea, rippling and shimmering like the water, wailing like the wind."

Indy listened for the strains of eerie music drifting over the silvery waters. Listened and watched. But he heard and saw nothing. The night was still and cool, and after a few minutes they each sat down, hunched against the chill, and waited. The moon floated slowly across the sky. Clouds came and went.

The cry of an unseen bird brought Indy alert. He couldn't tell which direction the sound had come from, or how far away it had been. A cool breeze suddenly touched his face, the caress of icy fingers. It was followed by the sound of flapping wings. Close by. Instinctively, he ducked, anticipating the pinch of talons or a beak against the back of his neck.

"What happened?" Fernandez asked.

"Didn't you hear it?" Indy leaped to his feet and looked around.

"Hear what? Music?" Panic laced Brody's voice.

"A bird. It almost hit me in the head."

"I didn't hear anything," Fernandez said. His hands were jammed in his pockets, his shoulders huddled against the cold.

Brody looked around uneasily. "I think we should get going. I'm freezing."

Indy peered into the darkness. He was sure he'd heard and nearly felt the flapping of wings. He turned his gaze to the sea. Moonlight still glistened across the empty, quiet waters.

"I don't think we're going to see anything," Fernandez said. "Not tonight."

As they walked back to the carriage, Indy mulled over what he knew and what he suspected. He separated the few facts from the conjecture. His conclusion was that islanders, at least a couple of them, had been abducted. But he doubted that a ghost ship was involved. It was something else altogether, and he thought he knew what it was.

He waited for Brody and Fernandez to catch up. "I'd like to talk with that old man you told us about."

Fernandez shook his head. "I'm sorry. That is impossible. Teotoro is dead."

"How did it happen?" Brody asked, keeping his eyes on the rugged terrain in front of him.

"He started complaining that he was hearing voices that told him he was going to be swallowed by a snake."

"Swell way to go," Indy said.

"He was so afraid that he tried to kill himself,"

Fernandez continued. "At first, he kept trying to drain blood from his body by poking himself with pins and putting leeches to his stomach. He even called the leeches by pet names. Then one day he slashed his arms with a razor. His brother was able to save him, but he didn't want anything more to do with Teotoro."

"I can certainly understand his sentiments," Brody said.

"What happened to Teotoro?" Indy persisted.

Fernandez stumbled, but Indy caught his arm. "He was taken to an insane asylum in Santiago, where he underwent a water cure."

"What's that?" Brody asked. "I've never heard of a water cure for insanity."

"He was doused in icy water repeatedly, then scalding hot water. Finally, he was wrapped tightly in wet sheets. "He underwent this horrible treatment several times a week until he died," Fernandez concluded.

"That is appalling," Brody muttered. "It sounds like something out of the Middle Ages."

Indy had the feeling that whatever had happened to Teotoro during the time he was missing was probably the same thing that Beitelheimer was experiencing right now. But then, if he'd been missing for years, how had he managed to send Brody a telegram?

Back at the hotel, Indy lay in the dark and waited for sleep. He kept hearing Fernandez's voice, talking about Teotoro's water treatment, and when he finally shut that out, the soft fluttering of the bird he hadn't seen haunted him. Over and over again, its wings pounded his body and its cry echoed in his head. He felt prickles on the back of his neck and realized that his shoulder muscles were tight and knotted.

He flipped onto his side. *Calm down,* he muttered. *Take it easy.* But no matter how hard he tried, sleep still evaded him. Finally, still feeling edgy, he tossed off the covers and turned on the light. It was two-fifteen. He wondered if the bar downstairs was still open. Maybe a shot of brandy was what he needed. He swung his legs over the side of the bed, and quickly pulled on his pants and shirt.

The bar was empty save for a single customer, a man who wore a hat and dark clothes. His head was tilted forward as though he were staring into his drink. Indy took a seat two stools away from him. As he ordered a brandy, the man lifted his head. His face was still shadowed by his hat. "*Hace frío esta noche,*" Indy said, commenting on the weather.

No answer. The bartender, a young man in his early twenties with thick sideburns, set Indy's drink in front of him, and glanced warily toward the other man.

"Leave us," the man said.

The bartender moved to the other end of the bar and busied himself washing glasses. The man ran a finger along the rim of his glass. "What do you want?"

"You talking to me?" Indy asked.

"You called to me."

"Who are you?"

The man turned and now Indy could clearly see his gray eyes and long face with its somber expression. There was something oddly familiar about him. Then he knew where he'd seen the face. It had been in one of the paintings on Fernandez's wall. A self-portrait by the artist.

"Well, well. If it isn't Hans Beitelheimer," Indy said. "Better known as Juan Barrios."

Barrios grabbed Indy by the front of his shirt, jerked him off the stool, and lifted him into the air as though he weighed no more than a sack of straw. "You are going to be dragged into hell. I see it in your eyes, Jones."

"What are you talking about? How do you know me?"

"By your mistakes. You made a big one, and now you're headed for the journey of your life. Pick the time. We are waiting."

With that, he dropped Indy back onto the stool, ripped open his shirt, and pressed his open hand against Indy's chest. It burned as if he were being branded, and he yelled out in pain.

Indy bolted upright in bed; he felt feverish and chilled. He flopped back down, rubbed his hands over his face, and muttered: "Go away. Leave me alone."

Bang. Bang. Bang. The pounding was relentless, and pulled Indy out of a deep sleep.

"Hang on. Wait a minute." He climbed out of bed, and crossed the room. "Who is it?"

"It's me."

Indy opened the door. "Marcus, what's going on?"

"You won't believe what happened, Indy. I got up this morning and went downstairs for coffee and there was a message waiting for me at the front desk. It's from Hans Beitelheimer. He knows I'm here. C'mon, get ready. We're going to go meet him in the plaza."

Indy rubbed the sleep from his face. "You mean he found us?"

"Apparently so. And we didn't even know we were lost!" Brody laughed, giddy with delight. "I'll meet you in the lobby in a few minutes."

As Indy ambled toward the bathroom, he saw that his undershirt was ripped and wondered how it had happened. He pulled it over his head and stared in the mirror. A red hand-print marked his chest.

"What?" He placed his own hand over the imprint, but the fingers were longer, thicker.

The bar. Beitelheimer. But that had just been a nightmare, hadn't it? He'd awakened in bed. He picked up his undershirt and saw that the fabric looked as if it had been shredded. He couldn't explain it. He looked at the mark on his chest again. It was lighter now, already fading.

As they headed toward the plaza, Indy told Brody about his experience at the bar.

"Are you saying it was a dream or that it happened?" Brody asked.

"A little of both, Marcus. That's the only way I can describe it."

"Well, if you don't mind, I'd like to see this mark on your chest when we go back to the hotel."

"It's gone. It just slowly disappeared."

Brody frowned at Indy. "This is all most peculiar. Hopefully, Hans will be able to shed some light on these matters."

The plaza was a hub of activity with vendors selling *empanadas* and fresh fruit. Some of the people milled about, others crossed the plaza intent on their own business. Brody craned his neck. "I don't see him yet, but maybe if we get ourselves a couple of *empanadas* and take a look around . . . Wait. I think that's him. Over there!"

"Where?" As Indy spoke, he glimpsed a tall blond man staring in their direction.

Brody waved and they moved ahead. They hurried through the crowd and were within ten yards of the man when Indy suddenly stopped in midstride and grabbed Marcus by the arm. "Look over there."

"What are you . . . Oh, my word!"

A man who looked identical to Beitelheimer, except that he wore a hat, was walking along a sidewalk toward the other Beitelheimer. "This can't be," Brody mumbled. "He's over here. Now where did he go?" Brody charged ahead, but the first Beitelheimer was gone.

Indy was more intent on locating the other man, but now he couldn't see him, either. Then he spotted the Beitelheimer with the hat hurrying through a crowd gathered in front of a vendor. Indy rushed after him, but two fishermen carrying coils of rope blocked his way. He dodged around them, but a rotund woman stepped into his path. He bounced off her soft fleshy girth, lost his footing, and tumbled to the ground. The woman's *empanada* fell from her hand and landed on the back of Indy's neck.

He wiped it off, picked up his fedora, and crawled through several legs as the woman berated him with a barrage of curses. On his feet again, Indy searched the square for the Beitelheimers, but didn't see either one of them. Brody came up beside him. "What in the world is going on here?"

"Good question, Marcus."

Brody wrinkled his nose. "What is that?" He reached into Indy's collar and pulled out a chunk of a hard-boiled egg coated with fried onions.

"Somebody's breakfast. I think she'll survive without it."

"Yesterday afternoon we were wondering if Hans was still alive," Brody said, struggling to put matters into perspective. "Now it seems as if there are two of him."

"And one of them was after the other one," Indy added.

"I'm almost positive the first one I saw was Hans. But I only got a quick glance at the one with the hat."

"Let's go down to the harbor and take a look around." They walked at a fast clip, but still kept an eye out for the Beitelheimers.

Gulls pinwheeled high overhead, riding the current of the ten-knot breeze that rippled the harbor waters. Most of the fishermen had already left for the day. The few that remained behind were repairing nets or working on their boats. Indy and Brody split up and started asking questions. Fifteen minutes later, they met at the base of the pier.

"Nothing," Brody said. "Nobody's seen Beitelheimer, and nobody wants to talk about the *Caleuche*, either."

"Ditto," Indy said. He looked around and saw several of the fishermen stealing glances in their direction. "At least the word should get around that we're interested in the ship."

Brody shook his head as they headed back to the hotel. "I don't know what to think. I don't mind telling you, I'm very confused right now."

"We're both a little baffled, Marcus. But we'll get to the bottom of it."

"I'm sorry to get you involved."

"Actually, Chiloé is turning out to be considerably more interesting than I'd imagined," Indy said.

They'd gone a couple of blocks when Indy noticed a couple kissing in a doorway. He could see only the back of the woman's head, but the man's face, with its thick sideburns, was right out of his dream. "Wait here," he said, and he walked over to the couple.

"Excuse me."

The man looked startled as he pulled away from the woman. *"Ahora, qué quiere?"*

"I just want to know one thing," Indy said. "Do I look familiar to you?"

The man stared at him. "How could I forget you? I had to carry you to your room last night from the bar. Please, don't get in any more fights with that ungodly seaman. The next time he'll kill you."

"Who is he?"

"Someone very strange. Evil. Don't look for him or his friends."

"What friends?"

"You are asking for trouble. They will find you before you find them."

The girl was still clinging to the bartender, and she looked frightened by what he said.

"Thanks."

"Now what was that about?" Brody asked.

"I just confirmed what I already was thinking. The Beitelheimer with the hat was the guy I saw last night, and it was no dream."

"What was it then?"

"A visit from a crew member of the *Caleuche*."

"A ghost from a ghost ship?"

"Not exactly. Let's get some breakfast, and I'll tell you what I think is going on here."

6

MARINERS

As soon as Indy and Brody arrived back at the hotel, they found a table at the restaurant adjoining the bar. Although Indy felt he had already had his fill of *empanadas* for the day, he ordered one anyhow, along with coffee. The waiter informed them that the restaurant was the only one in town that offered coffee, and a cup turned out to cost three times more than the *empanada*. But it was worth it.

"Indy, I know you want to get to the bottom of this matter with Beitelheimer as much as I do, but I don't want to delay your return to Easter Island. If you want to leave—"

"Marcus, don't worry about me and Easter Island," Indy interrupted. He'd already decided not to take the next ship leaving Santiago. "You got me here, and I'm not leaving until we've figured out what's going on."

"All right. So what's your theory?" Brody asked, stirring cream into his coffee. "I can't wait to hear it."

"My guess is that the *Caleuche* is as real as any other ship. It's probably a pirate operation. Simple as that."

"Modern-day pirates," Brody said. "An interesting idea. But what about the look-alike? How do you explain that?"

Indy sipped from his cup. "I'm not sure. But I always like to start with the most logical possibility, and go from there."

"Which means what?"

"I'd say Beitelheimer has a twin who's involved in the pirate operation. It's probably the reason that he came down here in the first place."

"But I never heard about any twin."

Indy shrugged. "Some people keep the black sheep in the family a deep secret."

"I suppose it's possible," Brody said, as their plates of *empanadas* arrived.

Brody picked up one of the meat pastries, bit into it, and mulled over what Indy had said. "Your explanation misses one big point," he finally said. "The ghost ship, or at least the legend of it, has been around for five hundred years."

Indy swallowed a bite of *empanada*. "Very tasty. Much better than the first one. I don't consider the age of the legend a problem. A ghost ship legend, complete with a crew of witches, was passed from one generation to another, and the pirates have just put it to their own use. No doubt they occasionally kidnap islanders for their galley slaves."

"You mean like Teotoro?"

"Right. Although he probably wasn't floating around on a ship for fifty years."

"I should hope not." Brody frowned, tapping his chin lightly with his index finger. "Well, you may be right. But do you think Beitelheimer is involved, or just this mysterious twin? And what about Fernandez's story about Hans seeing his wife on the ship?"

"I don't know, Marcus. It could be that the twin was trying to lure his brother into the operation. Or maybe Beitelheimer just lost his mind."

They were almost finished with breakfast, and considering what to do next, when an old man with thin, wispy hair and a three-day growth of beard cautiously approached the table. "You are the ones who were asking about the *Caleuche*?"

"That's right," Brody said.

The man looked around the restaurant, then back to them. "What do you want to know?"

"Whatever you know," Indy answered. "Sit down."

The man said his name was Antonio. His clothes were clean, but well-worn. His face was bony and interlaced with deep-set wrinkles. "These are evil times. Very evil. This past year has been the worst in my memory."

"Why do you say that?" Indy asked, doing his best not to snap at the old man. They needed specifics, not vague opinions.

Antonio leaned toward them. "The ones from the ship are active on the land, and many fear for their lives. They don't dare talk about the *Caleuche* to strangers."

"What about you?"

"I am eighty, maybe eighty-two. I forget. I don't have long here in this world, so I can speak."

"And what do you want to say?" Brody asked in a soft voice, as if he were the old man's confessor.

The man brought a pipe from his pocket, packed it with tobacco, and lit it. "When I was young and my parents were still alive, I saw the ghost ship for the first time. It was brilliantly colored and headed toward land one evening about twilight. My parents realized it was the ghost ship because they sent my brothers, sister, and me off to bed. But I disobeyed. I looked out the window and saw seven seamen approaching the house. They asked my father for supplies and water, and told him he would be paid in gold. And they wanted to use our house for a few days."

"What did your father say?" Brody asked.

"He told them that he'd rather be poor the rest of his life than give them even a drop of water. As long as he lived, he wondered why the crew never took reprisals. But they finally returned a few years ago."

"What happened?" Indy asked, thinking, *Now we're getting somewhere.*

"I still live in the same house, but now with my granddaughter and her husband," Antonio explained. "They are poor potato farmers like I was. But the crew gave them no choice. They were forced to make a pact. Otherwise, they would lose their children."

"What kind of pact?" Indy asked.

"They must leave their house at certain times and allow the crew to use it. Now is one of those times."

"You mean the crew is staying at the house right now?" Brody inquired.

The old man nodded.

"Will you take us there?" Indy asked.

Antonio puffed on his pipe. "I, too, am concerned

about the children. But I know that if nothing is done, those children will be haunted all of their lives by the ship and its crew. I will take you to the house tonight. They are getting bolder now. They must be stopped."

"Why do you say they are bold?" Brody wanted to know.

"Because I saw them capture a man this morning right in the street. No one dared stop them."

"What did he look like?" Indy asked, then exchanged a glance with Brody when Antonio described Beitelheimer.

"You must know something yourselves," Antonio said. "You were asking about the ship and a missing man."

"How do you know we're not from the crew?" Indy asked.

Antonio scrutinized each of them for a moment. "Because they don't act like you. They don't ask questions. They make demands and they act." He stood up. "Go to Chonchi, and wait at the hotel for me. I will meet you there at dusk."

He turned and walked away.

"We'll be there," Indy called after him.

There didn't seem to be many more automobiles on Chiloé than there were on Easter Island. But one old Model T operated as a taxicab in Ancud, and its owner gladly drove them to Chonchi. En route, they passed plowed fields planted with long rows of potatoes, and acres of coastal mud flats where women dug for clams. Clams and potatoes, Indy thought. And a ghost ship.

It was midafternoon when Indy and Brody arrived in Chonchi. The town was smaller than Ancud, and it didn't take long for them to walk around it. Several vultures were perched on the top of a two-story brick building near the waterfront, and three men, dressed in dark clothing, leaned against the wall, watching them.

The vultures, the men's stares, made Indy uneasy. "Let's go back to the hotel and wait for dark."

"Fine with me," Brody said. They turned around and retraced their steps.

No one had lit the gas lamps yet, and the dusk had consumed the dingy lobby where Indy and Brody waited. As if on cue, they both stood up when the door opened. A matronly woman, who worked in the hotel, stepped inside, and they were about to sit back down when Antonio followed her into the lobby.

"There you are," Brody said. "We were hoping you hadn't changed your mind."

"Are you ready?" the old man asked in a plaintive voice.

"As ready as we'll ever be, I daresay," Brody responded.

A cold drizzle had begun to fall with the approach of night. They climbed aboard Antonio's buckboard and headed out of town. The horse that was pulling them looked as old as Antonio and seemed to trot in slow motion.

Brody tightened the collar of his coat. "What sort of trouble do you think we're getting ourselves into?" he whispered to Indy.

Antonio, although old, didn't seem to have any problem with his hearing. He glanced at Brody. "Maybe they will be gone. I don't know."

"I hope we're not doing this for the fun of it," Indy

grumbled, tugging his fedora down so the cold rain didn't seep down the collar of his shirt.

"For many years, the ship was grounded, and we had no problems with it."

"Grounded?" Brody asked.

"It was in the shape of a huge tree trunk in a salt marsh near the village of Huidad."

"How did you know the tree trunk was the ship?" Indy asked.

"Because one day it just appeared in the marsh. There had been no wind the night before, and the sea did not reach that far inland. The trunk was ninety feet long and eighteen feet wide."

"Big trunk," Indy muttered.

"By noon, a flock of crows had perched on it and the villagers knew that it was the *Caleuche*. For ten years, the trunk and the crows remained there, until one day a crazy man came along and chopped into it."

"What happened?" Brody asked.

"It bled."

Sap, no doubt, Indy thought, dismissing the significance.

"That same night," Antonio continued, "the trunk vanished, and a short time later so did the man who had struck it with his axe."

Indy smiled, enjoying yet another Chiloé legend. But Brody was staring straight ahead, and from his forlorn expression Indy guessed that the museum director wished he were back in New York.

A few minutes later, they left the buckboard near a grove and walked to the top of a hill. Antonio pointed to a house near the base of the hill. It was so well lit that it looked as if it were on fire. A shadowy figure moved past one of the windows, then another, answering Indy's unspoken question. Someone was inside.

"How long have they been here?" Indy asked.

"Four days here, but they are other places, too."

Brody wiped the rain from his face. "What in the world are they doing?"

"Let's take a closer look," Indy suggested. They weren't going to find out much from up here.

"I'm too old to go crawling around," Antonio replied. "And it's not safe."

"I agree totally," Brody said.

"I'll go myself," Indy replied.

"But Indy—"

"It's best this way, Marcus."

Indy crept down the hill, watching for anyone outside the house. He stopped suddenly when he heard a growl, then slowly turned to see a large, black dog, teeth bared. "It's okay, boy. Take it easy."

The beast didn't look convinced. Then Indy remembered that he still had a stick of dried beef in his jacket pocket. He'd been carrying it around since the train trip from Santiago. He tossed it, and the dog caught it in the air with a snap of its jaw. Indy sidled away while the animal was occupied.

He bent down next to a window and peered inside. What he saw surprised, then confused him. The floor was covered with pails, and several men sat around a table busily working with knives, gutting fish, which were being brought from another room. From what he could see, the fish were all of the same species, a prehistoric-looking creature. Then he realized they weren't gutting the fish, but only removing orange masses of eggs from the females. The fish, which weighed between twenty and thirty pounds, were simply tossed on the floor.

No wonder the old man was angry. The house was probably going to stink of fish for weeks. *Real swell. I've uncovered some sort of fish-egg-gathering conspiracy. What are these guys, black-market merchants of the caviar industry?* Indy never did care much for caviar, and maybe now he knew why.

Some ghosts. They were as real as he was. Probably pirates who'd hit hard times, and were feeding on any trade where they could make a quick buck. It was no doubt illegal to harvest these fish eggs in international waters and that was why they were in the business.

Something cold, wet, and sharp closed over Indy's wrist. He instinctively pulled away, but the viselike jaws of the black dog held him firmly, yet didn't bite through his skin. "Easy, boy. Take it easy," Indy whispered as saliva ran over his forearm. "I don't have any more food for you."

The dog tugged firmly on Indy's wrist, as if to lead him away. Probably right into the pirate's den. But Indy quickly realized that if he wanted to keep his hand attached to his wrist, he had no choice but to go along with the dog. He scanned the ground for a rock or a board. A knockout blow was about the only thing that was going to free him.

But to Indy's surprise, the dog pulled him away from the house and into the darkness. About fifty feet from the back door, the dog stopped and tugged Indy down to the ground. Indy abidingly crouched; he glimpsed a man pacing back and forth in front of a shed. The dog let go of his wrist and whined.

"Is he guarding something, boy?"

The dog whined again and pawed the ground.

"Your master?"

The dog growled.

"Okay, let me take a closer look." Indy touched his whip, which was coiled on his belt. The guard wore a hat pulled low over his brow, but Indy recognized the hat and then the face. It was Hans Beitelheimer's twin. Indy crawled cautiously forward, noting that one of the other man's hands was wrapped in a cloth as if it were injured. But the dog didn't wait for Indy. It bounded past him, knocked the man to the ground, and grabbed him by his injured hand. The twin let out a howl, but he managed to pull out a knife and stab at the dog's head. The animal squealed, and as Indy fumbled with his whip, the guard stabbed at the dog again. The dog whimpered and dropped to the ground. The twin was about to strike a third time when the tip of the whip snagged the knife and snapped it away. The weapon dropped at Indy's feet. Only it wasn't a knife. It was a blunt stick.

Indy grabbed the man by the collar, and sank his fist into his gut. As the twin hunched forward, clutching himself at the waist and groaning, Indy caught him under the jaw with an uppercut, hurling him back onto the ground. The twin scrambled up, faster than Indy would have believed possible, and lurched toward him. The dog bounded between them, and flew for the man's throat. The man let out a choking yell, and fell to the ground under the dog's vicious assault. He flailed his legs and arms, then fell deadly still. And that was when Indy noticed that the guard's leg was shackled to a stake by a short length of chain.

He saw the man's face for the first time; it was Beitelheimer all right. But now he wasn't so sure which one. Indy leaned over the body. Beitelheimer's throat had been ripped out and his blood was soaking into the ground. Indy took a look at the hat. He was sure it was the same one worn by the man who had attacked him in the bar.

The dog growled in his ear. Stay on good terms with the dog; that was Indy's primary objective. He slowly stood up, backing away from the body. The animal leaped up, and Indy jumped back. But the dog was attacking the door, not him. Maybe Antonio's grandson had returned and demanded the house back, and the poachers had locked him up. But why was the twin shackled outside the door?

A massive steel lock held the door shut. But the hinges were old and rusted, and when Indy kicked it, the door rattled in its frame. He kicked again, and suddenly he realized he had no idea what the hell he expected to find. For all he knew, the shed contained nothing but dog food, or dead fish.

Then someone pounded from inside. Indy kicked again, and the screws in the hinges popped free and the door swung open. An angry voice shouted: "You have no right . . . no right . . ." The voice faltered, and a man stumbled to the door. Beitelheimer. The dog leaped up and lapped at the captive's face.

"Hans?"

"Who are you?"

"A friend of Brody's." Indy glanced around warily as he quickly introduced himself.

"Where is Marcus? I need to talk to him."

But Indy needed an explanation first. He pointed to the body. "Who is he?"

Beitelheimer dropped to his knees, and shook his

head. "My brother. The others were mad because I got away from him. So they forced him to guard me."

"All right. Get up. Let's go."

Beitelheimer patted the dog as they hurried away from the shed. "What's going on down there, anyhow?" Indy asked as they climbed the hill. "Why did they capture you?"

"I know too much, and now you know too much, too," Beitelheimer added.

"I don't know anything," Indy grumbled. "That's the problem."

When they neared the top of the hill, the dog growled as it sensed Brody and Antonio. Beitelheimer silenced him with a command that Indy didn't understand. Brody was elated to see Beitelheimer. "Hans, what in the world is going on here? I was terribly worried about you."

"Don't worry, Marcus," Hans said, shaking his hand. "I can explain."

Antonio backed away as he stared at Beitelheimer. His brow formed a deep furrow. He raised a shaky hand and pointed. "The one who was caught in the street injured his right hand. It was bleeding badly. This man's hand has no injury."

Beitelheimer turned to the old man. "You're mistaken. My hand was not hurt very badly." His voice was no longer friendly, but cold and piercing.

"He didn't mean anything," Brody said, stepping between them. "Let's go. We're all cold and wet."

But Indy remembered that the other Beitelheimer's hand had been bandaged. He reached for his whip. "Wait, Marcus. Antonio's right. This is the wrong one."

The man took a step back, and snapped his fingers.

The black dog darted to his side, bared its bloody teeth, and crouched, ready to leap. "Now you'll all die."

"What's going on here?" Brody demanded. "Just who are you?"

"You can call me Sacho. Now start walking."

The man appeared to be unarmed, but Indy had seen the dog in action, and the animal's gleaming eyes were fixed on him. The dog was the only weapon the man needed. "Down the hill," Sacho ordered.

"Wait a minute. If you're not Beitelheimer, where is he?" Brody demanded.

"He's dead," Indy said. "The dog killed him."

"Oh, no," Brody moaned.

The beast snapped at Indy's leg. He took the hint and led the way down the hill. Indy figured they were headed for the house, but at the bottom of the hill, Sacho directed them along a path which led toward the sea.

"Indy, where the devil is he taking us?" Brody whispered.

"Think about it, Marcus. Where did they come from?"

Before Brody could answer they reached a cliff. The water crashed against the rocks below them. If Indy still had any thoughts of getting away, they quickly were erased as he realized the night was alive with Sacho's buddies, the crew of the *Caleuche*. Dressed in black, they were barely visible in the darkness. As the mariners moved closer, Sacho stepped forward and grabbed Antonio by the back of the neck. "You broke the pact. You were not to talk. We warned you."

"Don't hurt the children, please," Antonio begged. "They are innocent. It is my fault."

"You're right, and you will pay." With that, Sacho flung the old man over the cliff. Antonio cried out, but he was quickly swallowed by the darkness and the crash of the sea against the rocks far below.

"Nice going. You killed an old man," Indy hissed.

"He knew what was waiting for him. Death was his only future."

"What are you going to do with us?" Brody asked.

Sacho turned his back to Brody and gazed out to sea. At first, Indy saw nothing. Then, through the mist, he glimpsed a golden glow. He squinted, and the glow took on the shape of a ship outlined against the night.

"The *Caleuche*," Sacho said.

"And it's not a ghost ship, any more than you're a ghost," Indy scoffed.

Sacho laughed as if Indy had said something incredibly hilarious.

A wave of rage flashed through Indy. "You think that's funny? Try this." He smashed his fist into Sacho's gut, but the punch had little effect. Indy was about to strike him again, this time in the jaw, but he stopped in midswing. The sight of Sacho's face stunned him. He was sure he'd been talking to the same man who had come out of the shack, the man who looked just like Beitelheimer. But that wasn't what he looked like at all. He had thick eyebrows, dark, narrow eyes, and a hawkish nose.

Suddenly, Indy lost his sense of certainty about Sacho, about the mariners, about the ship, about what was going on. Sacho took quick advantage of Indy's confusion. He grabbed his fist and twisted it until

Indy thought his wrist would snap. Slowly, Sacho pulled him closer until their faces were inches apart.

"You have no idea, Jones. No idea. I'm from a world that you don't believe exists. They call us ghosts here, but to us *you* are the ghosts."

7

ABOARD THE CALEUCHE

Tall men with long, dour faces and sallow complexions closed in on them. Their icy stares gripped Indy in a numbing chill. He backed away from them, but not too far. The edge of the cliff was just behind him, a lip of rock, and then nothing but the black, empty space where Antonio had fallen to his death.

Sacho raised a bony hand and pointed to the trail that wound down the ridge of the cliff to the shore. It was either follow it or get tossed over the ledge. "I think we'd better do what they say," Brody said.

"I always wanted to sail on a ghost ship," Indy muttered as they moved carefully along the narrow, slippery trail. Brody lost his footing as he maneuvered around a rock outcropping and Indy helped him to his feet. Indy glanced back; Sacho and the others seemed to loom over him.

When they finally reached the water's edge, Indy had a better opportunity to assess his captors. This time he realized they weren't all ghostly pale, nor grim-faced, nor tall. They varied in stature and features, and some were dark-skinned. Strange how the mind could play tricks. At first, it seemed the men had all resembled the haunting mariners of the myth. Yet, legends were usually based on certain truths, and the truth that was becoming readily apparent here was the part about the abductions.

The mariners forced them into a large rowboat, which had been sheltered by massive boulders. Someone shoved the boat from the beach, and the oars splashed the water. Indy noticed that the bow of the boat was filled with containers like he'd seen the men filling in the house. Fish eggs and pirates. Caviar and murder. *Swell bunch.*

But his attention quickly shifted from the boat to the ship, which came into view as they rounded the boulders. Lanterns were hanging from the rail every few feet, and there were more inside and along the mast, accounting for the luminous specter he'd seen from the cliff. It was a ship from another time, but it was still a real ship, and these guys were humans, too, Indy told himself. They had a few tricks up their sleeves, but he could deal with them as men much better than as ghosts. Besides, he had a few tricks himself.

The crew scaled a rope ladder to the deck, and the tall containers were quickly passed from one man to the next until they were all aboard. Finally, it was Indy's turn to climb the ladder. Only Sacho and Brody remained in the rowboat behind him. Indy's plan was already set in his mind as he stepped on the first rung. He yanked the rope which tied the boat to the ladder. He'd watched how it was tied, and knew it would come loose with a quick pull. Sacho yelled and grabbed for his legs, but Indy vaulted up two steps and out of his reach.

As Sacho lunged for him, Indy turned and dove into the churning sea. Sacho leaped into the water after him, and Brody grabbed an oar and stretched it out toward Indy.

"Row!" Indy shouted. "Get away from the ship." Sacho surfaced near him, and Indy plunged the mariner's head beneath the surface. But Sacho snagged Indy's legs and pulled him underwater. Indy kicked and fought to free himself, but Sacho wrapped his arms and legs around Indy, dragging him further down. Indy felt as if he were in the grasp of an octopus, and the thought made him literally swim out of his skin. He kicked loose, shot to the surface, gulped at the air.

The water was now alive with the crew as they dropped over the side of the ship. Brody frantically chopped at the water with one oar, and the boat turned in a wide circle a hundred feet from the ship. Indy swam toward Brody, windmilling his arms through the water. If he could climb aboard and get the other oar, they had a good chance of escaping.

He'd almost reached the boat when someone grabbed his ankle. He spun around, twisted, and flailed his arms as he tried to kick loose from the man's iron grasp, but to no avail. Brody came to Indy's aid, and slammed his oar down at the attacker. He missed, the oar harmlessly slicing the water. Desperately, Brody swung again just as Indy broke free of the man's grasp. It was a wild, reckless swing, and it struck Indy right on the forehead. Stunned, he slipped below the surface. His breath bubbled away;

water rushed into his lungs; the arms of death opened to embrace him.

His first memory upon awaking was the sound of creaking beams, the gentle sway of the ship, and the smell of the sea. Then he heard the distant music, an eerie, wavering sound like a calliope being played underwater. He was wrapped in something soft and warm like a cocoon. Maybe he was on the ship to the afterworld.

Indy rubbed his head and groaned. His lungs and stomach ached. He felt as if he had swallowed and inhaled several barrels of sea water. From the sour taste in his mouth, he must have puked it as well. No, he was alive all right, alive and hurting.

He heard a rustling sound nearby. Someone was here with him, but it was too dark to see. "Marcus, is that you?" he croaked. Every word was an effort.

"There is no one else here. Just you and me," said a soft feminine voice. A match flared, and a pair of emerald eyes glistened in the flickering light. Hypnotic eyes, he thought.

Indy tried to talk, but sputtered instead. When he stopped coughing, he managed to get three words out. "Who . . . are . . . you?"

The woman lit a lantern and held it up, illuminating prominent cheekbones and an aquiline nose. Her face was framed by dark bangs and copper-colored hair that was tied back in a single braid. "My name is Salandra. I brought you back."

"Back?" Indy propped himself up, and saw that he was wrapped in a thick blanket. "From where?"

"From the border of death. You were drowning

when they brought you to me. Actually, you had drowned. I brought you back."

He tried to clear the fog from his head, and think of the right questions to ask. "Who's playing the music?"

"You could say it is a ghost. It's the music of the portal."

"Porthole? Where are we? Is this . . ."

"Yes, you are aboard the ghost ship *Caleuche*."

He laughed, but then began to cough again, loud, hacking coughs that made his chest feel as though it were being crushed. Brody . . . he had to find out about Brody. "Where's my friend? We were together. He was in the boat when—"

"He is gone. He is not with us," Salandra answered in a solemn voice.

Indy's anger overcame his grogginess. "They killed him, didn't they? Just like the old man. Where is Sacho?" He pushed off the cot and managed to stand, but everything was spinning wildly, out of control. He lost his balance and toppled over. The air seemed thinner, like air in the mountains at some great altitude. Salandra scooped him up as if he were stuffed with feathers and laid him on the bed.

"You don't understand. Your friend was allowed to leave."

"Where are we going?"

"Questions . . . questions. Where, where, where. Just relax. No one will hurt you. Not while I'm here."

"Are you with these pirates?"

She laughed, a melodic trill. "What makes you think we are pirates?"

"Because you're not ghosts."

"You have so much to learn, and so little time.

Sleep now. You're safe here. When you wake up, we'll talk again."

It was becoming an effort to listen to her. With each word, he became increasingly drowsy. He struggled to keep his eyes open. "But . . . I need . . . to . . ." He fell back and into a deep sleep.

Indy stood at the railing and gazed into the thick fog. He was totally disoriented. Not only did he not know how long he'd been sleeping, but he couldn't tell whether it was dawn, dusk, or midday. He couldn't see more than a few feet in every direction.

He'd awakened a few minutes ago feeling astonishingly well, considering he should be dead. A lantern burned low in the cabin, and after getting his bearings he had hobbled over to the door. To his amazement, it was unlocked, and he walked out onto the empty deck.

Where was everyone? Why had he been left alone, the door unlocked? Maybe he should hide. Or jump overboard. But where was he? He couldn't see any land through the haze and faint light. If they were far from shore, jumping would be certain death.

"There you are," Salandra said from behind him.

Indy spun around. "Where did you come from?"

She smiled, but didn't answer. She was a long-limbed exotic creature with smooth, translucent skin. "How are you feeling?" she asked.

"Better."

"Good. There's a drink you must take while you're with us. If you don't take it, you'll get very sick and you'll die."

Sure. "I'm not drinking anything you give me. Now why don't you tell me what's going on. You can start by explaining what happened to my friend, Marcus Brody."

"I already told you."

"I don't believe that Marcus could have escaped in that boat. He couldn't even paddle it himself."

"If we had wanted him, he would've been easily captured. But he was of no consequence to us. We let him go, and he drifted back. By the time he reached shore, we were already gone."

Although she spoke English, it was with an accent that he'd never heard, and he had to listen closely to understand her. "What about me? What consequence am I? And just who . . ."

Indy heard voices, and three men appeared out of the fog. He tensed as they neared, but they passed with barely a look at him. They were arguing about something, or so it seemed from their gestures. But he had no idea what language they were speaking. As Indy watched the men disappear through the curtain of fog, he recalled his encounter with the mariners. "Who were they?"

"Just crew members."

"Wait a minute. What happened to Sacho? Is he here?"

"Of course."

"He killed an old man."

Salandra frowned. "You said that before. What old man are you talking about?"

"From the island. Sacho said a pact was broken, and that was the penalty. He killed Beitelheimer, too."

"Hans is dead? Are you sure?"

So she knew Beitelheimer. But unless she was lying she hadn't known he was dead. "Sacho's dog ripped out his throat." Indy was about to ask her what she knew about Beitelheimer when something else occurred to him. "How did he make himself look like Beitelheimer? What kind of trick was that?"

Salandra didn't answer immediately. She seemed to be mulling over what he'd told her. "Sacho is an illusion shaper; many Pincoyans are. He didn't actually shift appearances, he only made you think so. There's a difference."

"Nice to know. What's a Pincoyan? I never heard of them. Where are they from?"

"Pincoyans are from Pincoya. It is a region of islands. You will see it soon."

"I suppose you're one of these Pincoyans."

"My father is."

And your mother's a dolphin, he thought.

"And my mother," she began, as if reading his mind, "is from Wayua, a great desert."

Indy stared into the fog. He thought he was well traveled and well versed in geography, but he'd never heard of any of these places. Furthermore, he didn't want to see them, at least not against his will. "I'm ready to go back now. I think I've had enough fun for one day. Unless you can drop me off at Easter Island. That would save me some time."

She laughed. "Unfortunately, Jones, your work on Easter Island is going to have to wait. We need you."

"Need me? You've lost me. And, by the way, how do you know my name and about my work?"

She smiled. "If you would stop interrupting me, I might tell you."

In spite of himself, Indy couldn't help but return the smile. He didn't know anything about her, or about much of anything that had happened in the last few days, but he liked Salandra. It wasn't just that she was attractive, but there was something in her straightforward manner that suggested to him that she was trustworthy. But then again, deceit and treachery came in many forms, and he'd been fooled before.

"I am what you would call a private investigator," Salandra explained. "That's how I know about you."

Swell. A woman private investigator on a pirate ship that was disguised as a ghost ship. What else could he expect to hear? "I suppose you're going to tell me you've been hired by the ghost of a pirate who wants me to find his buried treasure."

The look on her face suggested that she wasn't sure whether Indy was serious or not. "It's much more complicated than that."

He couldn't help but laugh. "What in the world is going on?"

"That's well put," Salandra said. "That's exactly what I'm concerned about."

Indy shook his head. "You're not making any sense to me."

"I can understand that." She touched his arm. "I'm sorry you were forced onto the ship. But you came most of the way on your own. I knew that you would, from the moment that I found out Hans Beitelheimer had contacted your friend, Marcus Brody. Such a remarkable linkage. It was surely a sign left by the Great Mother herself."

"No doubt," Indy said, wondering who the Great Mother was. "How do you know Beitelheimer?"

"I've been following him."

"That's right. You're a gumshoe."

"But I got sidetracked and came upon you. That

was nearly a year ago. I followed you from your college to Easter Island, then to Chiloé."

"I'll have to take your word for it. I haven't seen you around any of those places. Who hired you?"

"No one."

"Then why were you following me?"

"Because I had to find out who you were, and how I could get you here."

"What's the point?"

"The point, Jones, is that you did something that must be rectified. You are the only person who can undo it. It is not only a matter of life and death. It involves the future of my world, and maybe yours as well."

My world, your world. Is this what happened to Beitelheimer and Teotoro? Am I losing my mind?

"I don't know what you are talking about."

Perspiration beaded on Indy's forehead. An overwhelming sense of dread swept over him, and he just wanted to escape back into sleep. He felt as if he weighed a thousand pounds and was about to puddle on the deck. Yet, he knew that she was prodding at something real, something buried away inside him, something he wanted to forget.

8

THE ALICORN

When she was certain that Jones was soundly asleep, Salandra prepared the nalca. She'd given him only a few sips of the drink the first time. Now he must drink more, especially since she knew he wouldn't take it on his own yet. His trust in her was growing, but he was not one who was easily swayed, and the drink remained well beyond the limits of his faith.

She sat down next to him. "You will drink this now," she said softly, and repeated the command. She lifted his head and held the mug to his lips. As he took a sip, his eyes remained closed. Then he took another, and continued drinking until the mug was empty. She laid his head gently on the pillow, and watched him sleep.

How could she explain anything about her world to someone who didn't believe that it even existed? She knew there was only so much she could tell Jones. He was a man who established his truths by what he saw, what he experienced, and what made sense to him. Everything had to be *verified;* that was the key word. When something didn't fit and couldn't be verified, he dismissed it to a corner of his mind where such things piled up for later consideration.

She had spent enough time in his world to understand Jones's way. He would be slow in accepting the reality of his new surroundings. He would look for other explanations. But in the end, she was confident that he would accept her world as real, every bit as real as his own.

She would have to be patient until he negotiated the new truth and accepted it. There was no choice in the matter. Jones's help was essential. She'd already discovered, much to her surprise and consternation, that she could do very little without him. Her thoughts turned back to the aftermath of Maleiwa's discovery of the alicorn.

After Maleiwa had abandoned the Channels of Paradise with his newfound staff, Salandra returned to Pincoya and informed her father about what had happened. He was concerned about Maleiwa, and wanted to know the meaning of the relic. Preventing the Wayua leader from expanding his power was of utmost importance. Salandra's father instructed her to go to Roraima where the great teachers resided, and to seek instruction. She had done so, entering the Tepui of Learning. But none of the teachers would help her. They told her that she was beyond their instruction, that she must act on her own abilities now.

But that wasn't what Salandra had wanted to hear. She needed specific directions. She needed answers.

Didn't they know this was important, that she wasn't a student any longer? Yes, they knew, and that was precisely why she must act on her own.

Finally, near despair, she climbed to the top of the tepui. There she had retreated to her dreams for counsel. At first, her dreams had been chaotic and confusing. None of them made sense to her. She had nearly given up and returned to Pincoya, when the Great Mother Rhea appeared to her in a waking dream, a dream that was not a dream.

Nothing like this encounter had ever happened to Salandra. Such visitations were mythical; they happened in stories, never to anyone she knew, only those she knew about, and they were from ancient times. Yet, now she knew the stories were true.

Mother Rhea appeared in the form of a woman, ageless and radiant in her beauty, and Salandra knew immediately in whose presence she was standing. It was nearly too much to bear, and at the same time she knew that the incredible being before her could only be a fragment of the true nature of the Great Mother. Anything more would be impossible for Salandra to comprehend or tolerate; her very existence would cease.

"The balance is threatened," Mother Rhea said. "You must get the staff away from Maleiwa, or all is lost. But beware, it is a sacred alicorn, a relic of power, and cannot be taken from him unless he willingly gives it up."

"But how can I stop him?" Salandra asked. "If it is so important, he'll never give it to me."

"The alicorn can be reclaimed only by one who has possessed it in the past. That is your answer."

Salandra was frustrated. She didn't know what to

do. Maybe Mother Rhea was simply testing her. Salandra had always used guidance wisely, but never
allowed it to limit her. She must find out for herself.
After all, that was one of the most important teachings
handed down by the Great Mother.

The image had no sooner vanished when, still in
her waking dream, Salandra shifted to the form of a
falcon, the bird which was her protector and her
wings. She soared high above the tepuis of Roraima,
over the forbidding Swampland, and onto the harsh
desert of Wayua. She spanned time and distance and
flew over the walls of Maleiwa's castle and through an
open window. She reshaped into her woman-form,
but not into full physical being.

She found herself in an alcove off of the castle's
main hall. She paused by the open door of the hall as
she heard sounds of laughter and loud talk coming
from within. Servants moved about clearing dishes
and bringing new platters of food.

Maleiwa was seated at the head of a crowded table.
He wore a long gold-colored tunic. His bronzed skin,
bald head, dark eyes, and strong features made her
recall their earlier friendship when they were both
students in Roraima. She wanted to walk inside and
listen to everything he had to say, but she'd come
here on a matter of great importance and her time
was limited.

She turned away from the feast and prowled the
corridors of the castle. She must find the alicorn. She
needed to see it again and learn everything she could
from it. She inspected room after room, with no luck.
Then a door opened just as she was about to pass
through it. A maid stepped out and locked the door.
The woman paused as she turned from the door,

tilted her head, and frowned. Then she shrugged and moved on. That one is perceptive, Salandra thought. She had sensed her presence.

Salandra walked into the room as the maid disappeared down the corridor. She immediately knew that this room was a special place for Maleiwa. It was filled with trophies from the warrior's many adventures. There were weapons of many sorts, and gold and silver artifacts representing beasts that were part human and part animal. Stuffed animals, including a huge desert snake and a fish with a head that looked nearly human, were displayed here and there in the spacious room.

Then she saw the alicorn. It was mounted on the wall above a massive desk. If the staff was such a powerful relic, why was it so exposed and housed with such worldly mementos? she wondered. She walked over to it and laid her hands on it. Usually in her waking-dream state, she could move physical objects. But no matter how hard she tried, she couldn't remove the alicorn from the wall.

Then, unexpectedly, she glimpsed Maleiwa as he had stood here placing the relic on the wall. She could hear his thoughts, as if he were speaking. He knew that the staff was a relic of power, but he already had power, he thought. It was nothing to him but a nice memento, a curiosity of the exterior world, even though its origin was no doubt the interior.

But Maleiwa thought more about this link and the nature of its power. The alicorn was a talisman of protection. With it, he realized he could pass through any of the gates to the exterior world, and no one could stop him. But the alicorn presented another possibility; he could use it as a lure to entice his ally to help him overcome the one big obstacle still preventing him and his army from taking up a long-term presence in the exterior world. He smiled cunningly as the plan took form.

Salandra heard it all. She had to get the staff away from Maleiwa and destroy it, to prevent his plan from coming true. She shifted to full physical form. Anyone walking into the room would see her now. But she had to take the chance. She pulled on the alicorn, then tugged at it. There was nothing holding it, yet it wouldn't budge.

Mother Rhea was right. She couldn't take it, and Maleiwa would never give it to her. How would she get it?

As soon as the question was posed, the answer came through the staff itself. She saw the man from the exterior world who had possessed the alicorn before Maleiwa. He was the one who had left it at the entry to the Channels of Paradise. He wasn't hiding it; he was giving it up, and that was why Maleiwa had been able to take control of it. She sensed who this man was, but she needed to find out more about him, much more, before she could approach him about the onerous task that would be required of him.

Salandra's thoughts returned to the present. She took one more look at Jones, then headed for the deck. So much depended upon him, and he was so vulnerable.

Sacho stood outside the door to the cabin as if he were guarding it. He bowed his head in the traditional Pincoyan motion of respect. "Is everything all right, Your Highness?"

She studied him a moment. "I was told that you

killed Hans Beitelheimer and the old man. Is that
true?"

He laughed nervously. "It was nothing. Just an illusion. I wanted Jones to fear me so that he wouldn't try
to escape."

She nodded. "You were convincing." Then she
pointed to the whip that was coiled on his hip. "And
what is that for?"

Sacho touched the whip and grinned as he nodded
toward the cabin. "I took it from him. They snap it
and beat animals with it." He made a motion with his
hand. "Sometimes people, too."

She would ask Jones about it. She couldn't imagine
him whipping animals or people.

"Make sure he is not disturbed until we reach the
port. He needs the rest."

He bowed again. "At your service."

I hope so, she thought. If she couldn't trust Sacho,
she was in deep trouble.

9

INTO PINCOYA

In the dream, Indy was a kid again, exploring Egypt with his father. They were walking near the Great Pyramid and his father was talking to a man with a flat-topped cylindrical hat with a tassel. Indy wasn't listening to what was being said. Instead, he was playing make-believe. The pyramids, the robes, the language, the music were all strange and exotic to him. He imagined it was another world and he'd traveled here by rocket as Jules Verne had done on his trip to the moon.

A door slammed. *We must be inside the pyramid now,* he thought. *No, that doesn't make sense. Pyramids don't have doors.* He came awake, and listened. Footsteps. Moving closer. Where was he? The ship. The woman.

"Salandra?"

He blinked. He glimpsed a form in the dark. Whoever it was had stopped a few feet short of the cot. "Who's there?"

The figure stepped closer, leaning over Indy. There was just enough light to make out his face. "Father? What are you doing here?"

No answer.

It couldn't be his father. He must still be dreaming, but it seemed so real.

"Hello, son."

It *was* his father, but it didn't make any sense. "What are you doing here?" Then Indy saw his whip in his father's hands. "Where did you find it?"

"Ah, Junior. You've left yourself vulnerable."

Indy started to sit up, but with the lightning swiftness of a striking rattler his father's hands looped the whip around his neck, pulled it taut, and kept pulling. Indy gagged as the whip cut into his throat. He grabbed his father's hands, but they were made of iron.

Wake up. Wake up. I'm dreaming. Indy gasped for air, gagging. Dream or not, he had to fight back, even if it was his father. He kicked his legs up, and the blanket covering him fell over his father's head. He broke free and rolled off the cot. He sucked in air, slammed his fist against the covered head, and tore away the blanket. As his father lurched toward him, Indy struck again, and this time his attacker's body went limp.

"Dad? Are you all right?" He gaped at the face, saw thick eyebrows and narrow, dark eyes. It wasn't his father at all. It was Sacho. But how could he have confused the two men?

Indy stood, but Sacho kicked his legs out from under him and straddled him like a horse, pinning him to the ground. Indy caught a glint of metal, saw that Sacho gripped a dagger, and suddenly bucked, hurling Sacho off.

Indy scrambled up, but Sacho was right behind him. "Sacho, no!" Salandra shouted. An instant later, Sacho fell back, arms pinwheeling, a dart protruding from his neck.

Salandra stood in the open doorway, holding a weapon that looked like a crossbow with no arrows. She nodded to the men who had gathered behind her. They rushed into the cabin and dragged Sacho's body away.

"He's not dead. Our weapons shoot darts that temporarily stupefy the target."

"Too bad," Indy muttered. He rubbed his throat, and wondered about the odd, bitter taste in his mouth. "You don't have guns?"

"No one can bring them from your world to ours. They don't exist here."

Indy didn't get it, but he didn't press the point. "I thought you said I wasn't going to have any trouble."

"I was wrong." She turned away from Indy. "Come out on deck. We're almost in port."

"Back in Chiloé?" Indy asked hopefully.

"No, Pincoya."

As she walked away, the impact of what had just happened to him struck home. Sacho indeed was an illusion shaper. He'd looked like Beitelheimer. Then he'd looked like Indy's father. Indy was in desperate need of an explanation, a sensible explanation of this nonsensical world he'd stumbled into. But right now it was more important to find out exactly where the ship was taking him.

When Indy reached the deck, the fog had lifted

and he could clearly see the ship and the surrounding sea for the first time. "You're going to have to show me this Pincoya on a map. I've never heard of it."

"I'll do better than that, Jones," Salandra answered. "I'll show you the city right now." They headed toward the bow until they reached a telescope that was mounted on a railing. Salandra peered through it, turned it slightly, and adjusted the focus. "There's Pincoya. Take a look."

"Okay, but I still want to know . . ." Indy stopped in midsentence as he stared through the scope. What he saw bewildered him. Even though the sun wasn't visible, it was light enough to see a city with numerous spires and towers in the distance. But it looked all wrong. It was as if the city was built on a hill with the buildings perpendicular to the slope. It gave the impression that he was looking down on the city from above.

He lifted his head from the scope and stared toward the horizon. He could barely see the city, but it looked as if it were floating above the sea. He saw a speck in the distance near the city and turned the scope slightly. He spotted a ship in the scope, but it appeared to be standing on end.

"I don't get it. It's some kind of mirage."

Salandra laughed. "I wanted you to see Pincoya before I tried to explain."

"What country is Pincoya in?" Indy asked.

"Pincoya. The city, the island on which it is built, and the entire region are the same. All Pincoya. Welcome to our world."

He turned away from his view of the city and peered at Salandra. "What is this about your world and my world? Unless we went to the moon when I was sleeping, we're both from the same world."

"No, we're not," she answered. "Yet, we are all one. That is what is most important."

"Tell me about it."

"Very well. Imagine a globe that is your world, and you can see all of the continents. Now slice the world in two at the equator, and look inside. In the lower half you see a bowl-shaped depression, and on this bowl you see continents, islands, and a great sea. Now if you were in that land, there would be no horizon as you know it, and the land in the distance would look as if it were turned on its side."

"Are you telling me that we're inside of the world?" Indy asked. "If you are, I don't believe it."

Salandra smiled. "You're going to find my answer to your question even more confusing, because it is both yes and no."

"You're right." Indy smirked. "I don't get it."

"A few years ago, you went into a jungle looking for a man who was lost. You found a city and many strange things."

"What do you know about that?"

"That city, Ceiba I think was the name, is like Pincoya. We are part of a legend and a dream. You could call us dreamers who are awake. In fact, that is our present condition."

"Well, if that's the case, I'm ready to wake up." Indy wasn't as interested in her analogies as he was in her source of information about him. "How do you know about Ceiba? Tell me that."

"I told you, Jones, I'm an investigator. I've found out a lot about you since you came to my attention."

A dozen questions popped into his mind. He still

didn't understand what it was he had done to deserve this free ride into a nightmare, and he was determined to find out. But before he could say anything more, they were interrupted by shouts from the crew as they scurried about.

"We're almost to Pincoya," Salandra said. "I'll be back in a few minutes," she said, and walked away.

They were entering a bay, and Pincoya was coming into view as they rounded a massive boulder. To his relief, the city appeared normal, with the buildings pointing in the right direction. Nothing seemed askew as his earlier glimpse had suggested, and he had to admit that Salandra's explanation, however outrageous, was one way of explaining what he'd seen.

The idea of a hollow earth was not unfamiliar to Indy. It permeated the beliefs and the legends of many ancient peoples. When Gilgamesh, the legendary hero of the ancient Sumerian and Babylonian epics, went to visit his ancestor Utanapishtim, he descended into the bowels of the earth. Orpheus also traveled there to seek the soul of Eurydice. After Ulysses reached the furthermost boundaries of the Western world, he offered a sacrifice so that the spirits of the ancients would rise up from the depths of the Earth and give him advice.

Pluto, who was also known as Hades, was said to reign over the underworld, and the early Christians believed that the souls of the damned went to live in caverns beneath the Earth. The ancient Egyptians thought the waters of the ocean flowed into the underworld, the abode of the dead, which was a mirror of the heavens. The Anasazis, Hopis, and other American Indian tribes believed that they had emerged into the outer world from an underworld.

But none of that mattered, Indy thought. Today, only crackpots believed the earth was hollow, and those who said they made visits to the interior of the earth ended up in asylums, and as far as Indy was concerned that was where they belonged. There had to be another explanation.

He took a closer look as they plied into the bay. It wasn't a fortified city like those dating back to the Middle Ages. There were no signs of walls to prevent an invasion from sea. Yet, the city didn't appear modern, either. The buildings were closely clustered together, almost as if the city were one huge building with many parts.

"I want you to meet my father when we go ashore," Salandra said as she rejoined him.

"Your father lives here? Is he a sailor?"

She laughed. "My father is the king. He rules this land."

Indy was taken aback for a moment. "I didn't know I was in the company of a princess. Or should I say a fairy princess?"

"Actually I'm what you would call a sorcerer and a healer. That's why you survived. When the men found your body in the water, you were as good as dead. I brought you back."

Swell. If he was to believe Salandra, she was a private investigator, a princess, and a witch doctor. What next, he wondered, but he decided to keep his doubts to himself. "Thank you," he muttered. "I'm always glad to be alive."

The ship had no sooner dropped anchor in the sheltered bay when they were met by several smaller sailing vessels. Maybe the *Caleuche* was a ghost ship to the people of Chiloé, but the Pincoyans didn't seem to find anything unusual about it. Indy also noticed that the crew treated Salandra with deference, which suggested to him that she might well be telling the truth, at least about being a princess.

As they stepped down to one of the boats, Indy saw containers of the fish eggs being loaded into a couple of the other vessels. "What do you do with all of the fish guts?"

Salandra sat down next to him. "We make *nalca* from the embryonic matter. It's the drink I've given you while you were asleep."

"*Nalca.* Tell me about it?"

"The eggs are from a fish which lives far below your southern continent in icy cold waters. Each spring the fish migrates north to spawn near the island of Chiloé. We go there to harvest the eggs." The city loomed closer as Salandra continued her tale. "You see, the same substance that keeps the fish from freezing far below Antarctica allows us and you to pass safely between worlds."

Here we go again, Indy thought. "What happens if I don't take your drink?"

"The liquids in your body will dry up and you will shrivel and disintegrate. So you must take a swallow of the drink when you pass through a portal and every few days afterwards, or face the consequences."

The boat eased up next to a pier. "If Sacho had told me about this drink, I don't think I would've believed him. I would've taken the chance that he was lying."

"Well, you had better believe me."

He didn't know quite what to believe. Or what to expect. He helped Salandra from the boat and they

headed toward the city. But he was as curious about
Pincoya as he was skeptical about the explanations
he'd heard. Hopefully, he'd make some sense of it all
when Salandra spilled her motives for bringing him
here.

They'd no sooner stepped from the dock when
three long-haired men in uniforms blocked their way.
Their clothing was of a sort that Indy had never seen.
They wore tunics and leggings that were shiny, silver
and shimmered like fish scales.

"Nice outfits," Indy said to himself. "Goes along
with the fish eggs."

The men each carried the same sort of crossbow
that Salandra had used on Sacho. He saw a slender
tube affixed to the bow, through which the darts were
shot. The weapon seemed to be a blend of bow and
arrow and blowgun.

"What is it?" Salandra asked tersely.

"Come with us," the brawniest of them said.

"Not until you tell me why," she answered.

"Your father is no longer the ruler here," the man
said. "He has fled to Roraima."

"I don't believe you. Get out of our way."

Salandra pushed through the men. One of them
grabbed her, and Indy slammed a fist into his gut. He
was about to land a second punch when he ducked a
wild swing from one of the other men. The blow
struck the brawny one in the jaw, knocking him
down.

"Thanks," Indy said, and he smacked the man in
the nose. "See ya around."

They dashed through a stone archway and up a
wide stairway to an open corridor which overlooked a
massive plaza. Indy was stunned by what he saw, and

momentarily slowed to take in as much of it as possible. The plaza was surrounded by buildings, which were not made of brick or stones, but were carved from a single gigantic rock. Then he realized that the entire city was a sculpture, hewn from a mountain. At the far side of the plaza, a waterfall spilled three or four stories over the top of the rock building, dropped into a pool, and apparently disappeared into an underground river. Surrounding the pool, and spaced throughout the plaza, were stone statues of strange creatures with human and animal parts. Men with antlers. Winged women. Fish heads and bird heads on human bodies. Some of them were doubles, with one strange creature stacked atop another. Moving among them were exotically dressed but perfectly normal-looking people. Two legs, two arms, one head each.

"Hurry!" Salandra shouted.

Indy glanced back and saw that they were being pursued, and raced after Salandra. They sprinted through more people, turned down another corridor, and dashed to a wide stone stairway. They descended several steps before Salandra pulled up short. Several more armed men waited at the bottom of the steps.

Salandra shouted to the crowd that had gathered. "Stop them. They are traitors."

But no one moved. The men raised their weapons. "Don't shoot!" Salandra commanded. "You know who I am." The men at the bottom of the steps wavered, then lowered their weapons. But Indy felt a stabbing pain in his leg, and saw a dart sticking out of his calf. The men who had chased them had fired on them from the top of the stairs. He pulled out the dart, and saw Salandra jerk one from her side.

"Nice try," he said, knowing that they were as good as caught.

"You won't get away with this," Salandra shouted. "My father . . . my . . ."

Indy dropped to one knee, and saw Salandra crumple over and tumble down the steps. He wanted to rush down to help her, but his legs wouldn't work; his body felt as if it were made of rubber. Darkness closed in around him; he heard a clamor of voices, then nothing at all.

10

MALEIWA'S MESSAGE

It was hard to say how much time had passed before the heavy door on the barren cell opened for the first time. Until now, Indy's days had been marked by the bowl of tasteless gruel and the pitcher of water that were shoved through a slot in the door. The light in his cell was faint, filtering through a narrow metal grid in the ceiling high over his head. There was no way to reach it, and no way to squeeze through it, even if he did. The only other hole in the cell was the one in the corner, his toilet, which was inhabited by rats and cockroaches. He slept on his cot from time to time, but never for long. Mostly, he paced across the floor of the twelve-foot-long, eight-foot-wide cell. Right now he wanted water. He'd drunk his supply and was still thirsty. He'd been pounding on the door off and on for the last hour, and was surprised when it finally opened.

Two guards filled the entrance, then moved into the

cell, his first visitors. They each grabbed one of Indy's arms, and he futilely tried to pull away from them. A third guard stood back with his dart gun ready to fire. "You want to walk or be dragged?" the one with the dart gun barked. He was a burly, fierce-looking man with broad shoulders, leathery skin, and white bushy hair. One of his eyes stared off at an odd angle, adding a kind of savagery to his already brutal appearance.

"Where are you taking me?" Indy asked.

"A new cell, with your friend."

"I don't believe you," Indy spat.

The guard pressed the dart gun to Indy's throat. "I don't care what you believe."

No sense fighting when there was nothing to gain, Indy conceded. He was taken down a corridor, then up a winding staircase. His feet barely touched the stone floor as the guards wisked him along.

Another door opened, and he was shoved forward. The door slammed. "Jones!"

Salandra leaped up from her cot, and hugged him tightly. The guard had told the truth, but what did it mean? At the moment, Indy didn't care. A warm tingling spread over him. The feel of Salandra's body pressed against him was worth every minute he'd spent in the cell.

Finally, she pulled back from him. "How do you feel?"

"Pretty good right now. You do know how to heal, don't you?"

"Are you feeling ill?"

"Just a little thirsty. That's all."

Salandra quickly picked up her pitcher of water, and Indy drank it all. "Sorry, I didn't leave you any."

"That's all right. We've still got time." She took him by the hand and led him to the cot.

"Time for what?"

Salandra wasn't smiling. "Sit down. There are some things I have to tell you."

"You can say that again," he said as he sat next to her.

They were in a circular cell with a single, barred window high over their heads. Indy guessed they were inside of a tower. "What happened, anyhow? No one's told me anything."

"My father has been deposed. He's in hiding in Roraima."

Indy had no idea where Roraima was, but it didn't matter. "Who deposed him?"

"Maleiwa. He's put traitors in charge."

"Who's Maleiwa?"

"He's the ruler of the Wayua. My father has been concerned about him. He was worried that Maleiwa's supporters had infiltrated our ranks and were stealing shipments of *nalca*. Now I know it's true, and Sacho must have been one of his couriers."

"Why is this Maleiwa so fond of fish eggs?"

"I've already told you that with *nalca* anyone can travel to the exterior world. But they must gain the consent of the United Council, and few win favor. Maleiwa, though, has been acting on his own. He's attempting to make a pact with one of the most dangerous men in your world, and thanks to you, he may have the bargaining tool he needs."

"Thanks to me? What are you talking about? I couldn't tell a Wayua from a Maleiwa."

Salandra touched a finger to her mouth. "Not so loud. They could be listening. I don't expect you to

understand everything right now, or even to believe
everything I tell you. But the reason you're here is
. . . the alicorn."

"What alicorn?" He already knew, but he didn't
want to believe it. He'd hoped he'd seen the last of
that thing, but he'd known that he might somehow be
touched by its poisonous legacy.

Last summer, Indy had gone to the American
Southwest to study Anasazi Indian rock art, and had
become entangled in a scheme to recover a so-called
unicorn's horn or alicorn, a staff made of twisted ivory
with a silver crest shaped like twin eagle heads. It was
an ancient relic that had been appropriated during
the sacking of Constantinople in 1201, and then was
kept for a couple of hundred years in St. Mark's Ca-
thedral in Venice. Much later, it fell into the hands of
an English family, who migrated to America. Great
luck and greater misfortune had come to each of the
owners of the staff, and finally it had been hidden in
an Anasazi ruin where Indy had recovered it.

"You left it at the entrance to the Channels of Paradise," Salandra said.

As if that explained everything, Indy thought. He
didn't really believe that the relic held any particular
power, but after a series of incidents in which he'd
narrowly escaped death, he'd decided to put it back
where he'd found it. No sense tempting fate, especially when it was his own. But he didn't know a thing
about any channels.

"I left an ivory staff in a crevice between two rocks
at the ruins of Hovenweep, in Utah."

"I know," Salandra said. "Then you set off an explosion that closed the entrance."

"Dynamite," Indy said. "How did you—"

"I saw it happen . . . from the inside. I'd followed Maleiwa without his knowledge, and saw him procure the alicorn."

Indy didn't know what to make of her story. Except that she did sound like a private eye. "So this Maleiwa has the staff, and he wants to make a pact. With who?"

"A man named Adolf Hitler. His people call themselves—"

"Nazis," Indy finished. "I've heard all about them. They're rabble-rousers, and they won't be around long. Hitler will probably end up in a looney bin."

"Don't be so sure. We have a better perspective on things than you do. Hitler will soon become the most feared man in your world."

"Right." Indy had heard a few fear-mongers say the same sort of thing. And yet he was curious. "So what kind of pact are you talking about?"

"Maleiwa wants scientists on the exterior world to create a drug which will replace *nalca*. He wants a massive, continuing supply so that he can bring an army into your world."

"This Hitler may be ruthless, but he's not stupid," Indy said. "What's in it for him?"

"Simple. Maleiwa will give him the alicorn, which will help Hitler gain great power very fast, faster than he would otherwise. It will seem as if there is no stopping him. And there won't be. At least, not until Maleiwa overpowers him. And that is his ultimate plan."

A familiar scenario, Indy thought. A stranger with some sort of powerful weapon befriends a warring leader, then the stranger turns on the leader. The downfall of the Inca Empire was a case in point. At the time of Pizarro's arrival, the empire was in chaos as two brothers fought for control. One of them accepted the help of the mysterious warrior from another land. But Pizarro soon turned on Atahúalpa, his ally, taking him into custody. He demanded a huge ransom for his release, then killed him after the ransom was paid.

All right, he'd play along with Salandra, as if what she said was true. "Has Maleiwa met Hitler?"

"Not yet. He's been using an intermediary, Hans Beitelheimer. He was Maleiwa's messenger and go-between. He told Hitler all about the interior world and promised him the staff."

"Beitelheimer?"

She nodded. "That's right. The man you were looking for. But Beitelheimer didn't follow through on his promise to Maleiwa. He was supposed to take Hitler to the interior world to meet Maleiwa. Instead, Beitelheimer went into hiding in the forest on Chiloé. But Maleiwa didn't forget about him, and his men caught up with him before you and Brody arrived."

"And now he's dead. So what's this got to do with me?"

"Don't you see? There are forces at work that on the surface look like coincidence, but there is deeper meaning and form to them. That is the way the Great Mother works."

"The Great Mother. Yeah."

"Let me put it another way. Your connection with the alicorn and with Beitelheimer, who was linked with Maleiwa and the alicorn, is no coincidence."

"Okay, what's it mean?"

"It means that you are the only one who can take the alicorn from Maleiwa."

Indy laughed. "I don't buy it."

Salandra touched his hand. "Believe me, if there was another way, I would've done it. I tried, and I couldn't take it, but I found out about you. The staff showed you to me."

"I suppose you believe in unicorns, too," Indy muttered.

"Of course I do. It's not a matter of belief. They exist. This world is where the unicorns are from. It's where all your myths and legends arose."

"I should've stayed on Easter Island. Tell me something that I can prove is true."

"I was getting to that. You need *nalca*, and soon. You've got only a short time left."

Indy wasn't impressed. "No one has given me any *nalca* since I've been in that cell, and I'm feeling just fine, all things considered."

"Jones, they were giving it to you in your food. But Maleiwa ordered it stopped three days ago. That's why you're here. He wants me to watch what happens to you."

Indy smiled. "You mean you're going to watch me dry up and crumble like a dried leaf?"

"I'm not joking. And there is more to it than I've told you."

"What more could there be?" he asked with a laugh. He rubbed his fingers over his arm. His skin felt dry. He realized his throat was parched. It was nothing, he told himself. False symptoms. His imagination.

"You don't exactly die without *nalca*. Your body reassembles in a place we call the Land of the Lost. The place between worlds. It's not a very pleasant

state of affairs. Once you're trapped there, it's virtually impossible to escape."

"Uh-huh."

Her skin seemed to tighten across her features and
her voice, although not angry, turned crisp and busi-
nesslike. "Look, Jones. I can appreciate your skepti-
cism. I even admire it. But spare me your sarcasm. I
don't have time for it."

"Hey, lady, all I want to do is get out of here." He
stood up, and moved around the cell. His joints were
sore. He ignored the pain. He tested the wooden door
with his shoulder, but it didn't budge. He shoved
again, harder. Nothing.

"Stay calm," Salandra said. "Don't use up your
reserves. There's a guard here who wants to help, but
he needs time."

Time, time, time, Indy thought.

"I told him where to find a supply of *nalca.* Unless
he has trouble, he should be here with it soon."

"And if he has trouble?"

She didn't answer.

Indy's mind raced at the possibilities. Maybe the
guard was lying. Maybe his friendliness had been a
ruse to see if Salandra would reveal more sources of
nalca. Maybe Salandra was a fruitcake. Maybe he
was.

"Listen!" Salandra hissed. Footsteps. The slit in the
door opened. Eyes peered in on them. The slit closed.

"Is it him?"

She shook her head. "I don't know."

A key jangled. The door creaked open.

A man who stood nearly seven feet tall stepped
inside the cell. His skin was brown, his head was
shaved bald. He wore a long, pale blue tunic that

reached midthigh and was belted at the waist with a wide strip of black cloth. His muscular legs were bare.

"Maleiwa!" Salandra's voice gave away her surprise.

His black eyes glistened. He spoke to her in their own language. "You should have listened to me long ago, Salandra. I told you my destiny would be to rule and to reshape our world . . . and his. But it's still not too late for you, Salandra. Join me. Your skills will be helpful on the outside."

"Give Jones some *nalca* right now!" she demanded.

Maleiwa laughed. "That is out of the question."

The only part of the exchange that Indy understood was his name and *nalca*, but he got the gist of it.

"What makes you think anyone will listen to you?" Salandra snapped. "They'll think you are crazy when you tell them who you are."

"I wouldn't be so sure of that." Maleiwa glowered at her. "Did you know that my father made contact before his death? I'll tell you exactly what they had to say about him."

Salandra didn't respond. Instead, she turned to Indy and translated their conversation.

"We can speak his language," Maleiwa said in the same peculiar English which Salandra spoke. He turned to Indy. "Salandra and I have both studied your people, but my exposure has been very limited. Salandra's father was responsible for closing the gate to my father after he made contact, and imposing difficult restrictions on all the Wayua."

"That was the United Council's decision, not my father's," Salandra said.

"He was the instigator."

One thought struck Indy. Maleiwa was going to his world, and in spite of Salandra's warnings, it sounded like the chance for a free ride. "Why don't you take me with you?" His voice cracked as he spoke. "I'll show you around New York. You'll get along just fine there. I guarantee it."

"Jones, you don't know what you are saying!" Salandra snapped.

Maleiwa glared at her, then smiled at Indy. "You don't understand, Professor Jones."

"Oh, yes, I do. You want to go to Germany and make a deal. Why bother with Hitler? He's not going anywhere. I'm sure the president of my country would be glad to start relations with your world. Have you ever gone to Washington, D.C.? Have you seen—"

Indy was babbling, trying to make some headway, but Maleiwa didn't buy it. He grabbed Indy by the collar.

"—Grant's Tomb . . . the Washington Monument?" Indy finished.

"You don't take me seriously. You think I'm a sideshow for one of your carnivals. You don't know who I am." Maleiwa reached inside his oversized shirt and removed a sheet of paper from an inner pocket. He handed it to Indy. "Read this. It's written by a man who started an organization in your world called the Golden Dawn. He not only knew of the interior world, but he was looking for us. This is what he wrote after several meetings with my father and those close to my father."

Indy unfolded the paper. The letter was addressed to the Members of the Second Order and was dated

1896, and it was signed by Samuel Mathers. He began reading aloud:

"As to the Secret Chiefs with whom I am in touch and from whom I have received the wisdom of the Second Order which I communicated to you, I can tell you nothing. I do not even know their Earthly names, and I have very seldom seen them in their physical bodies. They used to meet me physically at a time and place fixed in advance. For my part, I believe they are human beings living within this Earth, but possessed of terrible and superhuman powers.

"My physical encounters with them have shown me how difficult it is for a mortal, however 'advanced,' to support their presence. I do not mean that during my rare meetings with them I experienced the same intense physical depression that accompanies the loss of magnetism. On the contrary, I felt I was in contact with a force so terrible that I can only compare it to the shock one would receive from being near a flash of lightning during a great thunderstorm, experiencing at the same time great difficulty in breathing."

Indy stopped reading, and folded the letter. He wasn't impressed. He'd heard of the Golden Dawn and thought they were a bunch of misfits spouting madness. *And here I am, right in the heart of the madness.* He handed Maleiwa the letter. "I guess I don't get the same reaction from you as Mathers did from your father."

"Because you are in our world. I assure you that on the exterior, my presence will be felt in equally dramatic ways. But you will never know. You don't have very long left. When you are gone, Salandra's plans will be dead, too. Then I will personally visit your world and the man who is going to be my ally."

"What do you know of my plans?" Salandra snapped.

"I have my spies. I know you've followed me, and you've been reporting to your father on my activities. And I know you were going to use this fool to steal the unicorn's horn from me."

"Don't you realize the consequences of what you are planning to do?" she pleaded. "You will throw both of our worlds into total chaos."

"Salandra, I've spent my life preparing for the meeting of worlds. I'm fully aware that millions will die, but it's time for the people of both worlds to wake up. They've been sleeping far too long."

"I think you're out of your minds," Indy said. "Both of you. I don't believe a word of it."

Maleiwa ignored him. "I'll be back after you've watched your friend depart for the Land of the Lost. Then I'm taking you with me to the exterior, and you'll either cooperate or follow Jones into oblivion."

11

OUT OF PINCOYA

"Look, I'm sorry if I offended you," Indy croaked after Maleiwa had departed. "I guess I don't really think you are out of your mind. Maybe I'm the one who's crazy."

Salandra was seated on the floor, her forearms folded over her knees, her cheek pressed against her arms. "Don't apologize. There's no need for it." Then, raising her head, she added: "I brought you here against your will and that's a violation of our first law. I'm no better than Maleiwa. I deserve the same fate that awaits you."

Indy slumped down on the cot. He wasn't feeling so well. He needed more water, badly.

A few minutes later, the cell door creaked open again. This time it was the burly guard with the wild, white hair and the eye staring off into space. He looked as savage as a cannibal who'd missed his din-

ner, Indy thought, and wondered what was in store
for them now.

To his surprise, the brawny fellow stepped aside,
and a younger man half his size carried a tray with
two bowls on it into the cell. He set it down, and
glanced at Salandra.

The guard with the *nalca*, Indy thought. He'd come
through after all. The smaller man started to leave,
but the burly one grabbed him by the back of the
neck and slammed his head against the wall. The man
folded in half and crumbled to the floor.

Now what?

"Here!" The beefy guard stepped over to Indy and
handed him a pouch. "Drink. Now. Quickly."

Indy glanced up at him, took the pouch. He loosened the top and drank. Nothing here would surprise
him any more.

Salandra took the pouch from him. "Come. We
have to go."

They hurried down a winding set of stairs, following the guard. They entered another circular room
where several more of the long-haired, silver-clad
guards were posted. Their burly partner grabbed two
of the men, slammed their heads together, and released them. They crumpled to the floor. He grabbed
another one by the hair and cracked the man's head
against his knee.

One of the guards charged toward the door, but
Indy tackled him and they tumbled across the room.
Indy grabbed him by the collar, and was about to
punch him when he saw that the man was wearing his
hat. He slammed his fist into the man's mouth and the
guard keeled over. Indy grabbed his fedora and put it
on his head. "I'm feeling better already."

Another guard grabbed Indy's throat and throttled him. Just as Indy thought his neck was about to snap, a chair crashed over the man's head and the guard joined his companions on the floor.

Indy looked up at Salandra, who still gripped the chair. "Thanks." He looked around, then spotted his whip in the grasp of one of the unconscious guards. "You won't need this, but I might."

The burly white-haired guard unlocked the outer door. "Go!" he urged. "You can make it."

"What about you?" Salandra asked. Her brow was knitted with worry.

"I'll take care of myself. Don't be vexed. Your father will prevail." He turned to Indy. "Stay close to her. You need her as much as she needs you." With that, he pointed to the door. "Go!"

Salandra and Indy dashed out onto the open corridor that overlooked the great plaza. "Where to now?" Indy asked as he rubbed his neck.

"This way." She darted down a wide staircase to the plaza. They flew past one towering stone statue after another and headed directly toward the waterfall. The gushing water produced a mysterious musical resonance that swirled around them like the mist that was weaving webs of ethereal rainbows.

"What are we doing here?" Indy yelled over the sound of the water. It was hardly the time for a tour.

Salandra fixed the pouch to her side. She tested the knot, then looked over her shoulder. "Here they come! Jump!" she shouted.

"What? I'm not jumping in there. Are you crazy?"

A dozen uniformed men rushed toward them, crossbows raised and ready to fire. She grabbed his hand, leaped, and pulled him with her.

They fell through mist and water . . . and kept falling and falling. Salandra clung to his hand, but he couldn't see her, couldn't see anything. The fall seemed endless, and yet at some point he realized they were no longer falling, but rushing through the surging waters of an underground river. A powerful current hurled them forward. Indy gasped for breath as he bobbed up and down, and then the current pulled them beneath the surface.

When he was almost out of air, they burst to the surface, and before he could suck in a deep breath they were sliding over a slippery, smooth rock face that was covered by several inches of water. They careened along on a wild ride through the dark at an incredible speed. At times, Indy sensed they were actually rising, rather than falling. He expected to be slammed into a rock wall or a boulder at any moment. But nothing stopped them.

Then the bottom seemed to drop out of this embryonic world. Indy tumbled through blackness, head over heels, no longer grasping Salandra's hand. He struck water again, and plunged ten, fifteen, twenty feet. He kicked and clawed, then burst through to the surface, and gasped for breath.

Salandra. He called out her name. His voice bounced off a wall, echoing in his face. Something was different here. Of course: The water was calm. He was in a pool or a lake, an underground ocean, for all he knew.

"Salandra!" he shouted again.

"Indy! Are you all right . . . right . . . right?" Her voice reverberated from somewhere nearby.

"You're alive . . . alive . . . alive!" he answered.

"I think . . . think . . . so . . . so."

He paddled in circles, looking for her. He followed the ripples, reached out, and touched her arm. "Sounds like an echo . . . echo . . . chamber . . . chamber."

He laughed. He was giddy. They'd survived the fall. She joined him. They sounded hysterical, their laughter echoing around them. A house of horrors, he thought. "Let's swim . . . swim."

"Which way? . . . way?"

"Any way . . . way," he answered.

Suddenly, the water started boiling around them, its level rising, falling. "What the . . . what the . . ."

Salandra screamed. Indy felt something rub against him, and his hand touched a slick, rubbery surface. Then something wiggled between his legs. He nearly leaped out of his skin.

Salandra disappeared beneath the surface, then popped up again. "Indy, it grabbed . . . grabbed . . . me."

Fish didn't grab, they bit, but it was no time to argue. Then something gripped his leg and pulled. Indy reached down, and found a tentacle wrapped around his leg.

"I think it's an—" He was dragged beneath the surface, held there, released. "—octopus . . . pus," he shouted. Salandra was pulled under again, and as soon as she surfaced, it was Indy's turn. It was playing with them, like a cat with a mouse before the kill.

Suddenly, a massive mushroom-shaped body surfaced between them. An eye the size of a football stared at Indy. He punched it, and his hand sank up to his elbow in a quivering gelatinous mass, like warm mud. He was about to strike again when the creature started thrashing around, emitting a high-pitched sound, a whine, a shriek. Indy was catapulted with such force that he literally skipped across the surface like some large, flat stone.

He landed on his hands and knees in shallow water. He shouted for Salandra, and his call was answered by the same horrendous whine, which echoed all around him. He couldn't tell where the creature was or how far away. A wave sloshed over him. Something grabbed his shoulder and jerked him around.

"Jones," Salandra hissed. "It's me."

He hugged her.

"What did you do to that thing, anyhow?" she asked.

"I poked him in the eye."

"I think you taught him a lesson. He seemed like a little kid to me," she said.

"Same thing I was thinking. Let's hope he didn't go get Mommy."

They sloshed a few steps forward. The water was around their knees and it seemed to be getting shallower.

"Jones!" Salandra's voice was filled with panic. "I feel something spongy."

"Let's hope we're not standing on Mommy."

Salandra stifled a cry. "Something's crawling on my arm."

"It's probably just weeds. I feel it, too." He reached out, found her hand, and slid his fingers along her arm. He stopped as he felt something slick attached to her forearm. It was flat and larger than his hand. He grabbed the edge of it and pulled. It was like a huge suction cup. He held it up to his face so he could see it.

"It's just a leech. A big one."

"I've got another one," she said. "On my leg. No, two more."

He ran his hands over his own legs and arms, and started pulling off one leech after another.

"Oh, I've got them all over me," Salandra cried out. "Let's get out of here. Fast. I see land." She raced ahead, vanishing into the darkness.

"Wait a minute . . . minute," Indy called. He slogged after her, still pulling on leeches. He didn't see any land.

"Over here . . . here." Salandra's voice came from all directions. "Keep going . . . going," she said.

Indy took several quick steps, and the water level dropped to his ankles. Then he stepped onto a dry rock surface and felt something else beneath his feet: Salandra's slacks and blouse. "You must have jumped out of those clothes," he said, and laughed.

"It's not funny. Will you take this one off my back? Please?"

He reached out, touched her slick, wet hair, then found the leech. Carefully, he pulled it off, then tossed it toward the water. He shed his clothes, and went to work removing leeches. It was no time to be modest, and it was so dark it hardly mattered. He could barely see his own hand in front of him. When he was certain he'd found them all, he searched his clothing and squeezed out the water. He could hear Salandra doing the same.

In his concern about the leeches, he'd forgotten all about the other creature in the water. "That octopus wasn't too happy when we left it."

"We were lucky to survive. But, unfortunately, there's much worse in here. We are inside Minhocoa."

"Who or what is that?"

"A giant snake."

"A what?"

"Pincoya was built around the waterfall, which our legends say is a fountain for an enormous snake who guarded the doorway between worlds. There was a bad time in our history when sacrifices were made and many innocent people were thrown into the pool, and into the snake's mouth."

"I don't like being anywhere near snakes, much less inside one of them," Indy said.

"Don't take the legend literally."

Right. The fairy princess of the interior world tells me not to take a legend seriously.

"But there is some truth to the story," she continued.

"There usually is."

"You see, my father once told me that the legend served the purpose of discouraging our people from following these underground corridors to the exterior world."

"You mean this might be a way back to the real world?" He spoke the words slowly, trying not to get overly excited.

"The real world?"

"You know what I mean. My world."

"If we make it. The problem is that Minhocoa is the between-world. There is no way we can get to your world without first passing through her stomach."

"Her stomach?" He had a brief vision of himself being swallowed whole by a mythical snake, then being digested. "That's what you said? Her stomach?"

"In the legend, Minhocoa's stomach is the place you've already heard about, the Land of the Lost."

12.

CAVE WITHIN A CAVE

Whatever it took, Indy thought. Nothing was going to stop him from getting to a place that was even vaguely recognizable as the world he had known. His world was, or had been, one of considerable variety. Yet nothing he had ever seen compared to the strangeness that he had encountered in recent days. He couldn't even say how many days had passed since he'd been abducted in Chiloé. But that was the least of his problems right now.

"Do you think we're on an island?"

"No, it's a point of land, like a peninsula that runs into the lake. It rises from here until we reach a cliff."

Indy was puzzled. "How do you know? Have you been here?"

"I'm just telling you what I see."

"Are you kidding? I can't see anything."

"It's not so dark, at least for me. But my eyes are different from yours. They're more sensitive to light."

"Is that right." Indy snatched up his damp clothes, turned away, and started dressing.

She laughed. "I'm sorry. I thought you knew. It's time to move on."

"I guess there are certain advantages to being from Pincoya. At least in the dark." He recalled that he'd never seen the sun since he'd left Chiloé. It had been foggy or dusky when he was on the ship and in the city. "If you live in the interior of the world, as you say, where does the light come from?"

"We don't have a sun as you think of it. But we have illumination, like a continuous dawn in your world." She explained that it was created by electrical interactions between the earth's magnetic field and streams of charged particles, which bubbled into the atmosphere from bottomless pools heated by the core of the planet. "It's a phenomenon comparable to your aurora borealis."

"That explains everything," he muttered.

"Our atmosphere, of course, is different, too," she went on. "That's why you require the *nalca* every few hours while you are here, and I require it when I'm on the exterior."

He thought about what she'd just said, and realized that he was all set to trap her. "If there's no sun, Salandra, why do you talk about hours?"

She smiled and her emerald eyes seemed to grow larger. "It's true that we don't have a sun to guide us as you do in your world. However, we have an inner clock that is the equivalent of a twenty-five-hour day. By the time our children are three years old, they can tell the time within a minute or two. We also have an agreed-upon period of hours each day, which is for rest. Do you understand?"

"Sort of. So everyone sleeps at the same time?"

"Of course not. It's just like your world. No one has to sleep at any particular time."

She had an answer for everything, he thought. "Let's get going. I'll follow you, since you've got the eyes. In fact, why don't we tie my whip between us so you don't get too far ahead."

"Don't forget your hat," she said, after he fixed the whip around their waists.

He touched his bare head, then dropped to one knee and started patting the rocks.

"To your left," Salandra said.

He snatched it up and forced it down onto his head, and they started forward. They hadn't gone far before Indy felt a ticking sensation between his eyes. He lifted the fedora and yanked a leech from his forehead just as it slithered onto the bridge of his nose. He tossed it aside without missing a step.

As they continued on, he couldn't help puzzling over the mystery of Salandra and the interior world. He liked her, liked her a lot, and he really didn't think she was lying to deceive him. It was something else, something he couldn't quite grasp yet.

Light. That was what Indy wanted more than anything. The absolute darkness made him feel as if he were walking in midair. There was no context to anything around him. He had no sense of direction. If not for the gentle tug of the whip tied between them, he probably would've wandered off the cliff by now.

Salandra suddenly stopped, and Indy bumped into her. One foot slipped, and he tottered on the other. She grabbed his arm, then laughed. "It's all right.

We're well away from the cliff now, but we're going to be climbing soon."

"Soon? I thought that's what we were doing," Indy grumbled.

"I mean really climbing. There's a mountain ahead of us."

Indy stared into the darkness, and shook his head. In comparison to her vision, his head was covered with a thick blanket. "Any ideas what this stomach of Minhocoa looks like?"

"It's a labyrinth. That's what we're looking for."

"That's what *you're* looking for. I can't see my hand, and I don't know how I'm going to find my way in, much less out of a labyrinth."

"Here, take a swallow of the *nalca*." She held up her pouch; it looked like an oversized wineskin.

"I don't need any fish eggs. I feel fine."

"It'll help your vision. Besides, it gives sustenance. You won't feel any hunger for hours."

Indy swallowed the thick, viscous liquid, and wrinkled his nose at the bitter taste. Even though the *nalca* had taken care of his thirst and painful joints, he still had second thoughts about it. He had no idea what its effects were. But it was too late now.

The trail gradually turned rugged and steep, but he could see his surroundings now. Salandra was no longer just a voice. He could see her long legs striding forward, her copper hair, and her slender figure.

"It's getting brighter," he said.

"No, that's the *nalca*." She stepped aside, and he took the lead. As they climbed around boulders and picked their way along a rocky slope, Indy thought more and more about how much he wanted to get out

of this place and back to his life. "Do you have any
idea where we will be when we get out of here?"

"No, but I think it will be a sacred place."

"You mean like a church?"

"Maybe."

He imagined himself coming up through some
basement passage of a colonial church in a South
American capital. They would emerge from behind an
ornate altar trimmed in gold and pass by statues of
saints, the Virgin Mary, the baby Jesus. An organ
would be playing, and peasants would be kneeling at
pews in the dim light near luminous stained glass
windows. He'd walk out of the church and into a
world that, though it was hardly perfect, made sense
to him. He'd telegraph Brody that he was okay and
that he was headed for New York. Manhattan was
never going to look so good.

"What are you going to do when we get out?" he
asked, as he turned his attention to a ledge that ran
along a rock face. It started twenty feet above their
heads and curved up to a higher slope. If they followed it, they would save considerable time climbing
through a rock-strewn ravine.

"Go back through another gate. A safer one. I can't
stay in your world, not for long. Besides, I've got to
stop Maleiwa and I'm hoping you'll come back with
me."

Fat chance, Indy thought, as he looked for foot-
holds in the wall.

"Maleiwa is already disrupting the balance between worlds, and it's only going to get worse,"
Salandra continued. "It could get much worse. His
army would overwhelm your world in no time."

"Don't count on it. It's a big world."

"Maleiwa's warriors use fire energy. They can point a finger and burn a building or a person. They can move objects with their minds. It's a power that has many advantages, and your armies have no way of dealing with it."

"Let's get out of here first, before we talk about the future." He pointed to the ledge and told her his plan. He found a foothold, then another, and a handhold. The wall wasn't vertical, but it was too steep to climb without using his hands as well as feet. He slowly scaled the rock face, and as soon as he reached the ledge, he rolled over and reeled in the whip, gently assisting Salandra. When she was within reach, he grabbed her arm and helped her onto the ledge.

Indy looked out over the course they had followed. "I think we've got company." In the distance, he saw a pair of four-legged beasts scampering over the rocks. Then he saw several more. "Dogs. They look like the big black one that Sacho had in Chiloé."

"They must have been thrown into the waterfalls with orders to kill us," Salandra said.

"They look like they can climb pretty well, too."

"They're mountain dogs from Roraima. They will go right up this wall very easily. And once they are given orders, nothing will stop them."

"My four fifty-five Webley would slow them down. If I had it with me." The hounds spotted them and started barking as they bolted ahead. Indy doubted that the dogs could mount the wall, but he wasn't going to stay around to find out. He and Salandra hurried along the ledge until it vanished into a gently rising, rubble-strewn slope.

They stopped a moment; Salandra untied the whip. "We'll be able to go faster now."

The barking grew louder. Indy looked back just in time to see a dog take a running leap at the wall. It struck the rock face three quarters of the way up, and slid back down. He was relieved. Then a second dog leaped. One of its paws caught hold. It dangled a moment just below the ledge, then squealed as it tumbled down.

"Jones, over here!" Salandra pointed toward the ravine.

Four or five dogs had skirted the wall and were charging up the ravine. Without another word, they scrambled ahead, moving as quickly as they could. But Indy knew it was just a matter of time before the hounds caught them. There were plenty of stones to pelt them with and crack some heads. But if the dog he'd seen on Chiloé was any indication of the ferocity of the beasts on their trail, a few stones weren't going to save the day.

That gave him an idea. "This way." He turned toward the ravine.

"But the dogs—"

"I know. We're going to greet them." As they reached the edge of the ravine, Indy stopped by a boulder the size of a chest of drawers. He bent down low and shoved, but the rock was firmly anchored. He tried another one which was slightly larger, but not as well anchored as the other. Salandra pushed alongside him. The boulder wobbled, but wouldn't roll forward. The sound of savage barking pierced his ears.

"Jones, they're getting closer."

He shoved again. Nothing happened.

He grabbed a rock the size of a football, and hurled it into the ravine. It bounced twice, and struck a larger rock, which started to roll. "That's it. Small rocks."

They tossed one rock after another into the ravine, and suddenly it seemed that every rock on the slope was rolling. A cloud of dust rose, and the barking was swallowed in the thunder of the landslide. One moment Indy glimpsed the pack of dogs, then all he saw was dust and rocks.

They waited and watched. The landslide had moved beyond Indy's range of vision. The sound was a distant rumble. As the dust settled below them, there were no dogs in sight. "I think that did it," he said.

He'd no sooner spoken when he heard a low growl behind him. An icy chill raced from his neck to his toes as he turned and saw one of the black dogs crouched low on a boulder, baring its white fangs. Its sleek, fur-covered muscles stood out on its legs and shoulders. There was something predatory and almost catlike about the beast. Instead of simply leaping on them, as Indy would expect of a dog, this one was stalking them. Taking its time.

"I guess you're the high jumper of the pack," Indy muttered, as he cautiously unhooked his whip. He and Salandra slowly backed away, but they'd gone only a few steps when they bumped against another boulder. Indy was sure the dog was about to leap, so he cracked his whip. The dog snarled from its perch like a circus lion on a stool. Its ears were flattened back, but there was something oddly timid about its behavior. It seemed uncertain what to do. *Must be the whip,* Indy thought.

Another dog dashed into view from the ledge, fol-

lowed by yet another. He couldn't protect himself and
Salandra from this many hounds for long.

"Up here, Jones!"

He didn't dare turn away from the dog, but he
caught sight of Salandra on top of the boulder. The
other two dogs skidded to a stop a few yards away. All
three dogs were crouched and watching. Indy
couldn't understand their contrite behavior, but it was
the only thing keeping him and Salandra alive. "I
can't turn my back on them."

"Yes, you can. They won't bother you. I've be-
witched them."

So now she was a witch. He didn't feel a bit more
assured. He leaned back against the rock and inched
up the boulder without turning away from the beasts.
When he reached the top of the boulder, Salandra
had vanished from sight.

"Over here," she called. "Hurry. The spell won't
last very long."

She was standing fifty feet away, outside the entrance of a gaping hole in the mountainside. Indy
leaped down from the boulder, and they darted into
the mouth of the cave. The ceiling was high and
arched, and the passageway was straight and wide.
He was amazed that he could see anything, but his
vision was astonishing.

"What did you do to those dogs, anyhow? They
were acting like puppies."

"I reached into their minds and calmed them, but
they've been trained by Wayua. There's nothing gentle in their nature. They'll be after us in a few minutes."

"I guess you don't like the Wayua very much,"
Indy said as they moved on.

"I am Wayua." As if she'd never said she was from Pincoya.

"Now you're playing games with me." This whole thing was one big game. It was all about deception or perception, or both. "You told me—"

"I know what I told you. My father is from Pincoya, and my mother was from Wayua. They were both ambassadors to Roraima. That's where I grew up."

"That explains everything," he grumbled.

The corridor opened into a cavern. On the far side of it was a blue-green hole like a pool of water turned sideways. "What is it, another illusion?"

"The light and color mean we're close," Salandra said. "Your atmosphere reaches here."

"That's not exactly the way I remembered it looking," Indy replied.

"It wouldn't look the same here," she said as they crossed the cavern. "We're still in the between-world, and we've got a long way to go before we get out."

With every step it seemed that the green intensified and the blue faded. Indy slowed as he neared the end of the cavern. They were immersed in an emerald glow, and it was difficult to see clearly. But he had definitely been looking at a sky; a sky like none he'd ever seen.

"Which way is out?" Then he looked down, and was struck mute by what he saw. Beyond the hole was an abrupt drop, and a couple of hundred feet below them was a complex pattern of lines and squares and curves. At first, it reminded him of a ruins, a city without roofs. But then he realized he must be looking down on a vast labyrinth.

"There it is," Salandra said in a hushed voice. "The

Land of the Lost. We've found it . . . or maybe it found us."

"Why do you say that?"

"The legend says that the stomach of Minhocoa is inhabited with hungry beasts hunting for food. It's said they lure their prey to them."

"Yeah? What do they eat?"

"Lost souls."

"Swell." He tried to visually follow a route through the maze, but it was too difficult to keep track of the passages.

"Our only hope is finding a way to the other side," Salandra said.

"We'll do it." He didn't see what was so terrible about The Land of the Lost. It was just a maze. The rest was legend, and if there was a way out, they'd find it. Then, as he peered down at the steep grade, he saw it wasn't going to be quite as easy as he hoped. The maze began just below them.

"These rocks are all part of it," Salandra said.

"So I see."

He skidded down several yards until his feet jammed against the first wall. Salandra followed as he crawled over to an opening. He tried standing but it was too steep, and he started sliding down the corridor. He reached for a protruding wall to stop himself from crashing into a dead-end, then grabbed Salandra by the arm as she skidded by.

Another passageway cut across at an angle, and since it traversed the slope, they were able to stand and use the wall for balance. But the effect was distorting. They reached another pathway, and had to make up their minds again, as they would at every intersection. They decided to keep following the one they were on.

A mistake. It curved and led into a room with no other doorways. They backtracked, climbing up the incline, then found themselves trying to keep their balance as they followed another steeper route that headed off at a new angle.

Indy slid into a wall and caught Salandra in his arms. She hugged him. "This is confusing," she said.

"Agreed. Let's try this way."

"Why?" she asked.

"Because we haven't done it yet. I don't know. Got any better ideas?"

"Yes. Let's go straight down and climb over every wall we reach. We'll be at the bottom in no time."

Indy tugged at his fedora. "Why didn't I think of that?" He raced down the slope, no longer concerned about stopping. He quickly picked up momentum and as he neared the wall he leaped.

Even though it was about fifteen feet high, it was built perpendicular to an imaginary flat surface, rather than to the slope. That meant the top of the wall was considerably closer to his launching point. He clutched the top with both hands, pulled himself up, and swung one leg, then the other, over the wall.

He threw his whip down to Salandra, who was digging her heels into the ground to slow her advance. "Here, I'll pull you up."

She grabbed the whip. Indy had started to reel her in when he stopped, raised his head, and listened. Barking! "They're coming again."

He quickly pulled Salandra to the top. "Can you stop them like you did before?"

She concentrated; her eyes turned glassy. Then she

shook her head. "I didn't think it would work. They're smart. They blocked me. I can't do anything."

They dropped down to the ground, and raced for the next wall. Again, Indy easily leaped to the top, and tossed the whip to Salandra. This time, though, he saw a strange, frightening sight. The three dogs were leaping the walls with single bounds, and rushing toward them.

13

LAND OF THE LOST

They bolted over the next wall side by side. Salandra, spurred on by the dogs, needed no help. But now the ground was nearly level, and the walls were too high to climb. They darted through the maze, sprinting down one passage after another. Every time they reached a dead-end, Indy expected to find a dog blocking their retreat. But the hounds seemed no better at cornering them than Indy and Salandra were at finding a way out.

The barking suddenly intensified. The dogs were nearby, but he couldn't see them. Indy and Salandra pressed against the wall, uncertain which way to flee. Their only hope was that the confusion of passageways would befuddle the animals' sense of smell as well as sight. The top of a dog's head popped above the wall just opposite them.

"Did you see that?" he hissed.

"What?"

"That!"

Two paws snared the top of the wall, and a vicious jaw snapped at them. The dog's muscles quivered as it attempted to pull itself over the wall. Indy raised his arm, preparing to crack his whip across the dog's nose, when it let out a sharp squeal, and dropped out of sight.

Indy didn't wait around for an explanation. "This way!" They raced down the passageway, cut right, then left, then right again. He kept looking back, expecting one of the beasts to lunge out at any moment. He knew the dogs could attack from any direction. He and Salandra could be running toward trouble, rather than away from it.

They turned again, and then he glimpsed an opening in the wall at the end of a long corridor. Beyond the wall was a grassy field, with a dirt road crossing it. Indy could hardly believe what he saw: A '24 Ford, like the one he'd bought last summer, was motoring along, heading right toward the maze.

"Look!" he shouted. "Let's go." Indy rushed down the corridor toward the field. He could see a man wearing a hat in the driver's seat, and next to him . . . Indy could see the man's face clearly. It was his old buddy, Jack Shannon. What was he doing here? Indy was within a few steps of the field when he took another look at the driver of the car. He slowed. The field faded, and turned into a blank wall. Indy pounded his fist against it.

"Jones, what are you doing? What did you see?" Salandra asked, apparently mystified by his actions.

"Didn't you see it? It was a field, and a '24 Ford. Then they disappeared."

She shook her head. "I didn't see that. But for a

moment, I thought I was looking into my old room in Roraima."

"It's just another dead-end. I don't like this place very much. My best friend was in that car. So was I. Figure that out."

They backtracked until they found another passageway. Suddenly, the hounds snarled and growled, frenzied now as if they'd cornered their prey. But Indy didn't think the dogs were barking at him and Salandra. Then a wild, unearthly shriek cut through the air. It wasn't the dogs; it was something else. Something worse. The terrified shrieks collapsed into a single, ear-splitting squeal. A moment later, one of the dogs catapulted past them, and crashed against a wall.

"That was no jump," Indy hissed. "Something threw it."

"Let's get out of here," Salandra whispered. They edged away from the dead-end, while the terrible din of yelping, squealing, and wailing continued unabated. They were moving closer to the pandemonium, rather than away, but it was the only direction they could go. The clamor increased, and Indy felt that at any moment he'd be face to face with the devil himself. *Yeah, maybe that's where we are. Devils and snakes and the underworld do have a certain affinity.*

One of the dogs bolted around a corner and charged right at them. Indy snapped his whip, but the dog dashed past them as though they weren't even there. It ran directly at the dead-end corridor, and leaped the wall with the recklessness born of blind panic.

He glanced at Salandra, whose startled expression

no doubt reflected his own. "If I had three wishes, they'd all be the same. Out, out, and out of here."

They reached a corridor that was wider than the others. Indy recalled from his brief examination of the labyrinth from above that the wider trails cut directly across the maze.

He reached a corner, and was about to charge down the passageway when the last yelp died away. But the silence was as frightening as the clamor. He moved cautiously forward, expecting some ungodly creature to step into their path. Running would attract attention. So would talking. They did neither. Instead, they crept along and listened. The corridor curved, and Indy couldn't tell whether they were retreating from the scene of madness or heading toward it.

Then he found his answer as he spotted the dogs, or rather what remained of them. They'd been gutted and decapitated, their limbs strewn about. "I don't think you want to see this," Indy said.

Salandra was looking away, but not to avoid the sight of the disemboweled beasts. "Over here." She pointed at a trail of bloody footprints. They looked as if they'd been made by a hoofed creature. Indy studied the prints, then dropped to one knee and placed his hand, fingers spread, over one of them. The track was an inch or two larger all the way around. "This doesn't make sense. It's walking like a two-legged creature, and by the size of its hoofs, I'd say it's—"

"Jones!"

He couldn't look up. A frigid wind swirled around him, stroking him with icy fingers. It burrowed into his chest and prodded his heart. Then the wind dissipated, and Indy forced himself to look up.

The creature filled the passageway. Its eyes, a pair of burning coals, seared him. It stood nearly as tall as the walls. Its legs were covered with fur, its chest leathery and vaguely human-looking. Snakes slithered around its shoulders and neck. It had claws for hands, but its head was human, except for the horns above its forehead. It had a prominant hooked nose and beady eyes.

If this was hell, Indy knew who he was looking at. He slowly stood up, and backed away. The creature moved forward and sneered. It pointed at Indy. "English?"

The thing talked. "Yeah, English. I speak it."

"Fee, fie, foe, fum!" The creature laughed and growled at the same time.

"Thanks for taking care of the dogs," Indy said, knowing that what he said sounded ridiculous.

"No dogs allowed." It moved closer, and now the thing was a snake with a human head. "What are you doing here?"

"Looking for a way out."

"Maybe I don't want you to leave." It was back to being the furry devil-creature again. "Maybe I want you to stay here with me."

The beast rushed at him, its massive arms outstretched, ready to crush him. Indy's legs wouldn't move. He ducked his head, and raised his arms, but the collision he was expecting never came. He looked up; the creature was gone. He spun around. No sign of it.

Salandra gasped for breath. "What happened to it?"

"I don't know."

"Did you see its head?" she asked. "It had three

eyes, one on its forehead. And it spoke to me in my own language."

"What? It spoke English, and it didn't have three eyes. It had horns, but then it was a snake, too." He described the creature and repeated what it said to him.

She shook her head. "That's not what I saw or heard. It was the body of a silver bear, and it told me that my father was dead."

"Look at the tracks. They're hoofs, not paws." But now he saw that some of them looked like paw prints.

"But you said it was a snake, too?"

"I don't know any more what I saw, but we're lucky we didn't end up like the dogs."

They started down the passageway. "I think it responds to our thoughts," she said. "You saw the devil because you think you're in hell. I was told my father was dead, because I'm worried about him."

As they moved from one passage to another, a luminous green haze settled over the maze. Indy's vision was limited to about fifty feet, but the maze kept him from seeing much beyond that distance anyhow. "I'd say the creature was just a hallucination, except I saw what it did to the dogs."

"The dogs got just what they intended for us," Salandra pointed out.

Indy peered down another passageway. "I wish I had a map of this place."

"We had a map when we looked down on the maze. Remember?"

"It didn't do much good. I couldn't even see across it. But where is the mountain now?" If they could find it, they could orient themselves. The mountain was in the one direction Indy knew for certain that they didn't want to go. He peered up into the thickening haze, but the air was quickly turning into green pea soup.

"I think it's over there."

"That way," Salandra said at the same time. Their fingers crossed each other. "I guess one of us is turned around."

"Or both of us," he conceded as they continued on.

"I'm getting tired. I think we should rest," Salandra said after a while.

"In here?"

"Do we have a choice?"

The thought crossed his mind that they might never get out, that he would die in this maze at the hands of some terrible creature, or simply from lack of water. "You know all that water we were drowning in earlier? We don't have any of it with us. Not a drop."

"We've got *nalca*. It'll take care of the hunger pangs and keep us from dehydrating."

"Swell. Caviar for breakfast, lunch, and dinner."

They came to yet another dead-end, a small room just large enough for them to stretch out. "What about right here?"

"I don't know," Indy said, warily. "It leaves us trapped if something comes along."

"If something comes along while we're sleeping, it won't matter. Besides, if there are other creatures in here, they're less likely to find us here than in a main passageway."

"I guess you're right," he conceded. "We wouldn't want to sleep over on Monster Boulevard."

"At least you still have your sense of humor." She opened her pouch.

"Do they have humor in your world?"

"What a silly question. We are every bit as human as you are."

"From what you've told me about it, your world is nothing less than a legend. That's the only way I can describe it."

"And this place is a legend to my world as well as yours," she said.

Indy sipped at the *nalca*, handed the pouch back to her, then spread his jacket across the hard floor so they could both rest their heads on it. "I hope this stuff doesn't keep me awake all night, or whatever time of day it is."

Salandra lay down next to him. "The *nalca* isn't like coffee. But it is sometimes used as an aphrodisiac."

He heard the softness in her voice, and wondered if her remark was an invitation. His eyes shut, and he drifted, riding a sweet tide of sensations: her mouth nuzzling his neck, his hand stroking her hair, their clothes melting away. His blood raced, with *nalca*, with passion.

Salandra. The name was running through Indy's mind as he came awake. Somebody from a dream. He'd worked late last night studying a Rongo-rongo inscription that was etched on a wall, and had slept in the cave. He sat up. Bits of the dream came back to him. Something about another world, a maze, strange creatures, dogs . . . making love. A whole jumble of things, none of which made sense any more.

Indy walked through the dimly lit passage. He wanted to take a look at the inscription again. Thanks to Davina and Raoul, he felt as if he were on the verge of cracking the text.

He stopped in front of the wall, where six-foot-tall creatures, half man, half bird, were etched on either side of the text. He stared up at the stylized plants and animals of the Rongo-rongo script. For a moment, Indy wondered why the wall was so well lit, since he didn't have a lantern with him. But then it didn't matter. The script was all that was important. He understood. At last. It made sense. Everything he'd been working on came together. He could read it!

The first people to populate Te Pito o Te Henua arrived from the underworld. Finding this new land was a great discovery. It was the first Gate to the exterior world. More and more people soon arrived. Boats were built, and many of the people sailed in search of other lands. But Te Pito o Te Henua remained forever the Navel of the World.

"Jones!"

Indy's concentration was interrupted by a woman's voice calling out to him. "Davina?"

He turned in a circle. Where was she? He couldn't tell which direction the voice was coming from. He took one more look at the engraved glyphs on the wall, then moved down the corridor, turned once, then again.

"Jones?"

The voice was more distant now. Something wasn't right. He wasn't sure where he was now. He must have taken a wrong turn. But that wasn't all. Davina never called him Jones, but someone else did. "Davina?"

No reply. He touched his hand to the smooth wall.

Why was it so smooth? And what was the source of this odd, greenish light?

The dream. It had something to do with that dream. Then, slowly, it dawned on him. He must be sleepwalking. The dream was real. "Salandra?"

14

PROMISES TO A MAZE

"Jones?" Salandra called out again.

Where did he go, and why hadn't he woken her up? She was getting anxious. She would wait a couple more minutes, then go looking for him. She hoped he hadn't strayed too far. The last thing she wanted to do was go wandering around this labyrinth by herself.

She had needed the rest, but her sleep had been tortured with images of Maleiwa rising in power and destroying the delicate balance between worlds. The Nazi leader, with whom few were now concerned, would gain power at home, then quickly expand his base. Hitler was fascinated with magical powers, and his intent was to pervert them for his own selfish purposes. Maleiwa knew this fact, and that was why Hitler was the ideal ally.

The Invisible Alliance, as it would be known, would afford Hitler everything he needed. He would consider the Wayua warriors of the interior world fearsome and perfect, and he would want his people to breed with them. With the power of the unicorn's horn in hand, and the warriors of the interior world at his side, he would be invincible. Until Maleiwa revealed his true intentions.

Salandra had to convince Jones not only to return with her, but to go after the alicorn. Without it, Maleiwa would have a much more difficult time luring Hitler into an alliance. But she knew Jones would fight any attempt to take him back to her world, and she wouldn't force him. It would do no good.

Hurry, Jones. I can't lose you now.

She had to stay calm. She leaned against the wall and crossed her arms, as she turned her thoughts away from her predicament. She smiled as the memory of her recent tryst with Jones came to mind. Their passion had been furious and desperate. It was as if the danger they faced had intensified their desire. Yet, Jones had been tender and considerate.

She looked up as Jones stepped into the entryway of the room. "There you are," she said, relieved. "For a minute, I thought I had lost you." She stepped toward him, but something kept her from hugging him. "I was getting worried."

When he didn't respond, she asked if he was all right. "Jones, say something."

He stared straight ahead, zombielike. He raised a hand, pointing at her. He opened his mouth, but no words came out. Then he faded . . . and vanished into the green haze.

"Jones!" Salandra rushed up to the spot where he had stood, and felt an icy chill in the air. It wasn't him at all, but an apparition. This place couldn't be trusted. They had to get out. Her abilities were weak-ened here. She had stopped the dogs, but that had been accomplished only with considerable difficulty, and the effects had quickly worn off. She felt powerless and at the whims of forces she knew little or nothing about.

She raced out of the room, her wild titian hair flowing behind her. She paused as she reached another passage. She glanced both ways, and tried to call out Indy's name again. But her throat was constricted and the words were barely audible. She bolted down one of the corridors, turned again. She sprinted to the next crossing point, and spun around. Corridors headed off in five directions. She had no idea which way to go, or even which way to return to the room. Salandra was lost, and she panicked.

Her mind shrieked: *Out of here, out of here. Now. Now.*

It was bright, very bright, and Salandra was in a place that was vaguely familiar. It was the university where Jones was teaching, and she was following him along a crowded walkway toward a building. It was the first time she had seen him, that is, the first time since she had held Maleiwa's alicorn and glimpsed its former owner. She had gathered enough about him in those few moments to trace him. And here she was, wondering how she would convince him to join her.

He'd barely walked into the building when several students surrounded him. She moved closer to him, and heard the students asking him about his summer. Jones kept walking as he talked about studying petroglyphs in the Southwest.

"Did you find anything really important?" a pretty woman asked.

"*I wasn't digging for artifacts, if that's what you mean.*"

"*Was it exciting?*"

"*Some of us find rock art exciting, but most people would be bored.*"

"*I heard you got in a fight with someone out there,*" another young woman said.

Jones slowed, but just for a moment. "*Now where did you hear that?*"

She laughed. "*I didn't. I just made it up.*"

"*Very funny,*" Jones said. "*Excuse me.*"

What about the unicorn's horn? Salandra asked the question silently. But the professor heard it clearly. He stopped, turned, and peered at the faces around him. She stood several feet behind the group and could see Jones's startled expression. But he didn't look past the students to where she stood.

"*Something wrong?*" one of them asked.

A couple of beats passed. "*No, nothing's wrong. I have to go. My class is about to begin.*"

She knew then that he was not going to be easy. He would never believe her, not unless he saw things for himself.

Suddenly she was no longer on the campus. She was on Easter Island where she had soared as a falcon from a plateau on Roraima, eclipsing the distance in seconds. It was night, and Jones was walking along a beach. Water glistened under the moonlight and lapped at his feet, as he headed toward the distant glow of a camp fire where other people were gathered.

He glanced to one side as he heard the screech of a bird. Jones walked a few more paces, then stopped and looked around. He sensed her presence. He shrugged, moved on.

"Don't let Marcus Brody down," she said as Jones approached the fire. *"That's all I ask."*

The image abruptly shifted again. Now she was dreaming of herself and Maleiwa. He was tall and muscular, with chiseled features, a hawk nose, and dark, piercing eyes. His head, which in later years would be shaved, was covered by short-cropped hair. It was a time when they were students in Roraima. They stood at day's end near the edge of a tepui, looking out over the rugged landscape far below the plateau. Salandra nearly forgot that she was reliving a memory.

They were both outsiders born of another land, and that had brought them together. Maleiwa had been sent to Roraima because he showed a particular talent for legerdemain, and Roraima was the place to study the weirding arts. He was talking passionately about a particular aspect of their studies referred to as shadow-thaum, which concerned the manipulation of events and people. He was trying to convince her of the value of what he was doing. It was a subject that was considered outside the realm of practice, but one they were required to study nonetheless.

Supposedly, they were learning the detrimental effects created by those who had abused their powers and used them to control people. But Maleiwa was enthralled by those who had ruled through such means. He actually seemed to revel in how they had violated the first rule of conduct they were taught: Nothing by force.

"Don't you see the possibilities, Salandra, if we apply shadow-thaum to the exterior world?"

"That would upset the balance. It can't be allowed. You know that."

"I know that the events of our world are in sympathy with those of the outer. One reflects the other. What we do affects them. What they do affects us. There is balance."

"Maleiwa," she said patiently, *"force only encounters resistance, and nothing is ultimately accomplished but further displays of force."*

He laughed and told her that she sounded like one of their teachers. *"You know your lessons well,"* he'd chided. *"But I'm learning the true nature of power, and how to put it to one's own best use."*

After that day at the edge of the *tepui*, they were never close again. She didn't trust Maleiwa's motives. When his education was completed, he returned to Wayua and rose in power so rapidly that she was almost certain he was practicing shadow-thaum.

The image of Maleiwa faded, but now Salandra's inner vision was flooded with a barrage of other memories of the Wayua leader. Salandra recognized she was dreaming, and when she did so, she willed away the images. She was a skilled dreamer, after all, and she could stop or change a dream at will.

But to her great consternation, she couldn't control the thoughts and images. They sped by rapidly, and they were somehow associated with a keen intensity of feeling that she didn't comprehend. She prodded and poked into the depths of the dream as only one with her abilities could do, and there she found something totally unexpected, and nearly beyond comprehension.

The dream-thoughts were not for her benefit; they were triggered by another being that had invaded her innermost thoughts. She reached out with her mind and touched the other. The contact was momentary, but the shock of it jolted her down to her very essence. Her heart nearly exploded from acute fright.

"Salandra!"

She was back in the maze, and Jones was rushing at her down a corridor, several of him racing down several corridors. They converged on her from all directions. She squeezed her eyes shut. They grabbed her and shook her, and she screamed. None of it was real.

"Salandra, it's okay. I'm here."

She opened her eyes. There he was, one Jones. "Is that you?"

"Of course it is. What happened?" He stepped back from her.

"This place. It's . . ." She rubbed her arms.

"I know . . . I know. It's enough to drive you nuts."

"It's not what it seems."

"What is it? That's what I'd like to know."

"It's alive. It's a being that thinks. I touched its mind. It's studying us. It wants to know what we were doing here."

Jones looked around. "Yeah? Well, I'd like to know that myself. And, listen, call me Indy. Okay?"

Indy. The name rolled through her mind like a round, polished stone. Indy. "We're in great danger unless we somehow appease this thing. We'll never find a way out."

"What does it want?"

"I don't know."

Then she caught a fleeting glimpse of something large as it crossed the passageway. "Indy, did you see that?"

"What?"

"That!" It stepped out into full view, and she felt a blast of heat so intense that she thought her skin would melt and her blood would evaporate. She nearly wilted under the onslaught. Then the heat vanished as quickly as it had arrived.

The creature looked as if it were a blend of a huge cat and a man. Its head was humanoid except for the large green cat eyes and fangs. The lower half of the body was that of a massive cat. The upper torso was human on the underside, but its back, arms, and paws were distinctively feline.

The cat-man moved closer. "Your dreams tell all."

"What do you want?" she asked.

"A favor. In return you can leave me."

"What?" she asked.

"Send this one called Maleiwa to me."

"How can I do that?"

"Find a way. There are many routes leading here."

"And if I don't succeed?"

"I will find you through your dreams and destroy you from the inside out."

"How do we get out of here?"

The creature didn't answer. Instead, it turned and walked through a wall as if the wall didn't exist.

"What in God's name was that thing?" Jones asked.

"An image projected by the mind of the maze." Salandra described what she had seen. She wasn't surprised when Jones said that he'd seen something else altogether.

"It looked like a gigantic frog with a human head," he explained. "Enormous black eyes, a wide, flat nose, and hardly any lips."

"I made it a promise, so we could get out of here," she said.

He laughed. "Yeah. So did I. I told the thing that I'd stick with you until you kept your promise. What did I get myself into, anyhow?"

Salandra didn't want to remain another second on the spot where the apparition, or whatever it was, had appeared. She started walking, as she told Jones what she had pledged to the creature. Neither of them thought about where they were going. They turned down a passageway without questioning their choice, and she wasn't sure which of them was selecting the route.

"If Maleiwa is anything like you've described, that doesn't sound like such an easy promise to keep."

"We'll do it. Somehow."

They'd reached an intersection of three trails, and stopped. Jones pointed down one of the branches to a low, diamond-shaped opening. "What do you see down there?"

"A hole in the wall."

"So do I."

"Let's see where it goes."

They didn't rush for the hole, nor did they take their time. Both of them kept their gaze fixed on it, believing it would suddenly disappear if they looked away. Salandra knew that if the labyrinth was still playing games with them, she could do nothing to prevent it. Yet she reached deep inside herself, focused her intent on the hole, and willed it to remain in place.

Jones dropped down to one knee and peered into a dimly lit chamber. "It seems to lead outside of the maze."

The hole was barely large enough for Jones to squeeze through. Salandra quickly followed. Their eyes adjusted to the dim light. The earth smelled richer, and the air was more dense. She was certain that they were now just below the surface of the exterior world.

She glanced over her shoulder at the wall. "Look, Indy! The hole's gone."

"I don't want to know about it," Jones said, and didn't look back.

She touched the spot where they'd crawled through. It was as if the hole had never been there. Then she patted it as if it were a pet. "We're on our way."

15

BACK IN THE REAL WORLD

Even though they were still underground, Indy sensed something was different. Oddly enough, he almost felt at home. Thick pillars of earth appeared to grow out of the ceiling and floor, creating a series of archways. They entered a larger chamber, where the light was somewhat brighter, and the walls were painted with a red-and-black rhomboid design. The diamond-shaped figures reminded Indy of the opening in the wall they'd passed through to get here.

"Look at this, Indy!"

Salandra was peering into a niche carved into the wall. It contained calcified bones, bones that looked human. Below the niche were rows of clay vessels, painted with the same red-and-black geometric design as the walls.

"We're inside an Indian funerary chamber. Off-hand, I can't identify the culture."

"It's from your world," Salandra said as she loos-

ened the top to her *nalca* pouch. Even though he was
hungry and thirsty, she didn't offer him the pouch,
and he didn't ask for it. Right now he was looking
forward to eating real food. A beer or two sounded
like a good idea, too.

They found another chamber, and more skeleton-
filled niches and pottery. Indy was fascinated by what
he saw, but more than anything he wanted to get
outside. The next chamber was the brightest of all.
They crossed the painted room to where three steps
led upward. Indy's excitement, though, abruptly
turned to wariness. The light was tinged green, as it
had been in the maze.

He climbed the steps, hoping they didn't lead into
another maze, or back into the same one. Something
blocked his view at the top of the steps, and for a
moment he expected to see another creature. But it
was a bush. Or he hoped it was. He touched it, and it
didn't change shape. It felt like a bush, and gave off a
familiar acrid odor of plant life.

"Indy?" Salandra called.

"I'm going up."

He pushed his way through the thicket, which
thoroughly blocked the entrance to the chambers, and
squinted as the bright sunlight struck him full in the
face. He warned Salandra, who was following close
behind, to shield her eyes, then hurried out, anxious
to see where he was.

They were on the crest of a mountain, with a view
of green, rolling hills and tree-filled valleys. It looked
more familiar than anything he'd seen for some time.
He glanced up toward the blue sky and sun and he
smiled. He had never been so glad to see a sunny day.
He guessed it was midmorning. Back into the familiar

cycle of time, he thought. He'd never realized how much he would miss it; he'd always taken day and night for granted. But never again. Then he spotted smoke curling up from a rooftop lower on the mountainside; smoke, a familiar symbol of home.

"Do you know where we are?" Salandra asked.

"Can't say I do. But let's go introduce ourselves to the natives and find out."

They climbed down from the ridge and made their way toward the smoke. Within an hour, they reached a field of neat rows of bushes covered with small dark red berries. Indy picked one of them, and smiled. "Coffee. Hey, maybe we're in Colombia," he said, laughing. But there was no way they could've traveled across the South American continent so quickly, even if he'd actually taken an underground route.

They soon came upon a modest wooden house with a thatched roof, and were met by the yelps of a couple of dogs. Compared to the dogs they'd already encountered, these two were nothing to be concerned about. The door opened as they neared the house, and an elderly man and woman stepped outside.

"*Buenos días,*" Indy said.

The man answered the greeting. At least Indy had guessed the right language. He explained that they'd been hiking in the mountains and had gotten lost, and could they direct him to the nearest town.

The old man eyed him warily. "Where did you start your walk?"

Not a good question. Indy feigned that he misunderstood him. He waved a hand toward the mountain. "We're from the States."

The farmer looked up at the mountain as if it would offer an explanation. Then he murmured something

to his wife, who answered by saying they were foreigners, as if that explained everything.

The old man pointed down the mountain. "We are
closest to the village of San Andrés de Pisimbala."

The old woman smiled, touched Salandra's arm,
then motioned a hand to her mouth. *"Tiene hambre?"*

"Si, claro," Salandra answered, adding that animals
had gotten into their food last night, eaten everything,
and destroyed their pack.

Clever, Indy thought as they headed inside, and
wondered why Salandra spoke Spanish so well.

The old woman heated up a thick potato-and-
chicken soup, which they ate with clumps of fresh-
baked bread. It was followed by steaming cups of
coffee with frothing milk on top. At the moment, Indy
could think of nothing that compared to the satisfac-
tion he felt from eating the simple meal.

By the time they finished, they'd learned that the
closest city was Popayan, which meant they were in
Colombia. There was no logical way Indy could explain how they'd gotten here, but he didn't care.

Once they got to Popayan, they could catch a train
to the northern coast, probably Cartagena. Indy figured he had just enough money stashed in his boot,
along with his passport, to make the trip. Once they
were in Cartagena, he'd wire Brody for money for a
boat trip to the States.

He could just imagine how Brody would react
when he saw the telegram and realized that Indy was
still alive. But maybe Brody wasn't back in New York
yet. Indy hadn't been gone that long. That could be a
problem. But he'd work something out.

"We better go," he said to Salandra. They thanked

the couple, and Indy asked the old farmer about
transportation to Popayan.

"You can get a ride from one of the farmers going to
market, but it might take a couple of days. In March
through June there are wagons every day with their
coffee beans. But in September . . ." He shook his
hand in a gesture indicating that it wasn't such a good
time to catch a ride.

"September? But it's still June, isn't it?"

The farmer stared at Indy, then said something to
his wife about crazy foreigners. "Today is the third
day of September."

"He knew that," Salandra said, patting Indy on the
shoulder. "He likes to joke." They all laughed and
parted ways.

As they headed down the mountain to the village,
Indy felt as if he'd been run over by a tank. "It's not
really September, is it?"

"Time is different in the interior world," Salandra
began. "You experienced an expansion of time. What
seemed to occur in a matter of days actually took
much longer."

"I didn't sleep enough to be gone that long," he
grumbled. "It doesn't make sense."

"I know it's confusing. You see, you don't remember everything. You spent nearly three weeks on the
Caleuche before we reached Pincoya. Then we were
imprisoned for more than a month before we escaped.
It's hard to say how long we were in the between-
world. But I'd say it was at least a week in the maze
alone."

She had to be kidding. "You're right. I don't remember it that way."

"But it's true, and now you know."

"Why didn't you tell me the truth?" He was angry with her. "You let me believe I'd only been there a few days."

"No, I didn't," she said patiently. "I told you how we perceive time in the interior, but I didn't say anything about how *you* would perceive it," she continued. "I knew it would've only confused you even more than you were."

At least there was one advantage to the sudden shift in time, Indy thought as they continued walking toward the village. Brody would most certainly be back in New York by now. He wondered if the museum director was spreading the story that Indy had been abducted by a ghost ship. If that was the case, Indy's disappearance might soon rival that of Colonel Fawcett, the English explorer whom Indy had searched for in the Amazon.

"Sorry I lost my temper back there," he apologized.

"It's understandable," Salandra answered in a quiet voice.

"Where did you learn Spanish?" he asked. "You speak it like a native."

"I travel in your world often," she answered. "And I'm good with languages, like you."

He was still skeptical. "Why do you travel so much?"

"I am just one of a group who is dedicated to preserving the delicate balance," she answered. "It's part of my healing practice, you could say."

"You mean the balance of your world and this one?"

"My world and yours, and also the earth and the cosmos."

"Sounds like a big balancing job."

"It wouldn't be so big if there was more coopera-
tion. There are too many like Maleiwa and your
Hitler, who will rise further in power whether
Maleiwa helps him or not."

"Don't associate him with me. You told me you
were a private detective when we first met."

"I am that, too, thanks to Maleiwa, and you."

"How do you know that Hitler is such a threat?"
Indy asked.

"The pattern is set. I can see it. It's just a matter of
how it will be carried out, and how far he will be
allowed to go."

They continued walking in silence along a trail that
wound through shrub-covered hills. Indy thought
about the promise he'd made in the maze to stick
with Salandra. But he'd made it under duress, and
in his book that meant it didn't count. Besides, he
wasn't even sure who or what had solicited the
promise.

Then again, he didn't want to hurt Salandra. He felt
an attachment to her. Not love. No, it wasn't that. He
didn't think he would ever love anyone as he had
loved Deirdre, the wife he had lost three years ago in
the Amazon. There would never be anyone like Deirdre. The tenderness he had shared with Salandra was
no doubt born out of the baffling and frightening experiences they had stumbled upon. But the closeness
they felt now wouldn't last. Besides, as Salandra
freely admitted, she was from another world, and she
would go back.

"You will go to Roraima with me, won't you?" she
asked. "I have to find my father, and you know I need
your help getting the alicorn."

"You want me to go back into that maze?" Indy

exclaimed, astonished. "After what we went through to get out of it? No, thanks."

"I don't mean back that way. There are other portals that eclipse the between-world. Besides, I'd like you to meet the Gatekeepers."

"The Gatekeepers?"

"They live in your world. They are born here and live their lives here. They are in this world, but not of it. They will tell you more about the two worlds."

He was about to question her about the Gatekeepers when he remembered his strange dream in the between-world in which he had found a wall covered with Rongo-rongo script, and easily decipered it. He told Salandra about it. "It said that Easter Island was a gate between worlds. The first gate."

"That was not an ordinary dream," she responded as they continued toward the village. "What you read was true. In a sense, Easter Island is the navel of the world, because it is a gate."

"But there are many places in the world that the ancients called the navels of the world—Delphi, Stonehenge, Chaco Canyon in the Anasazi territory, to name a few," Indy countered.

"Of course. Those are all primary gates. Just like the one near Orongo on Easter Island."

"You sound like you've been there."

"I went through it when I visited you."

"I don't remember any visit."

"It was brief. You might have noticed me as a passing bird."

"Guess I didn't recognize you." He'd come to expect the unusual from Salandra, and her comment hardly surprised him.

The trail curved and the village came into view

below them. It looked as if it consisted of a single street, with a few buildings on each side. Indy was wondering how long they would have to wait for a ride when he noticed a stone statue a short distance from the road.

They walked over to it. The stone figure was about six feet tall, and its face looked part human and part feline. Its eyes were those of a cat, its mouth was filled with animal teeth, and its hands were claws.

"It's like the thing I saw in the maze," Salandra said. "Cat and man."

"I'd guess it's a jaguar-man. It's a common theme in myths and legends from the Amazon to the Andes."

"What do you think it means?" she asked.

"I've heard it said that the feline god represents the conflict between forces of good and evil," Indy answered.

"Look, there are more."

They moved to the next statue. "An owl with a snake in its beak," Salandra said.

"It looks more like an eagle to me than an owl. But I guess it doesn't matter. Both of them symbolize light and power."

They walked slowly past three other statues. All of them showed anthropomorphic features. A lizard-man, a snake-being and a frog-thing. The latter two were similar to Indy's own visions in the maze.

"How do you know so much about these creatures?" Salandra asked. "Have you been here?"

"No, but I've studied the myths of the region."

"Do your books tell you that these mythical beings are inspired by the underworld?"

"Not in the sense that you mean."

"The between-world we traversed is the home of

many mythical creatures. But in my world, they are myth and fact."

They walked over to the next statue. It was another jaguar-man, but this one was different. Mounted on its back was a second figure, which also possessed similar feline qualities. Its head was directly above the lower figure.

"It's known as a double," Indy said.

"Yes, I know. We have a few like this in the Great Plaza in Pincoya. They have a secret meaning."

Indy vaguely recalled the statues in the plaza. Pincoya and the interior world already seemed distant, and truly otherworldly. "I don't think anything is so secret about it. I'd say the top one is some sort of divinity or spirit guide."

"That could be," Salandra said. Then she added: "But there is more to it than that."

"Tell me about it?" Indy was annoyed by the way she talked around subjects sometimes, as if the knowledge would be too hard for him to comprehend. "Are mythical beings like these worshipped in your world?"

"The stone images aren't worshipped. Each one holds a certain meaning to us that represents part of what we are. Seeing these figures here reminds me that we are all one at heart."

"I guess you can see all kinds of things in them. They remind me of my profession, and I'll be glad to get back to it," he responded.

As they returned to the road, they saw a horse and wagon approaching from the direction they'd been walking. They waved as they recognized the old farmer. He pulled on the reins of the two horses, and the wagon rolled to a stop. "You want to go to Popayan?"

"We sure do," Indy said.

"Then you drive the wagon for me. I want to visit my son, who lives there. But I get too tired."

"I'll be happy to drive." Indy helped Salandra aboard the wagon, then took the reins as the old farmer slid over on the bench. He realized he didn't know the man's name. They'd eaten at his house without even exchanging names. He introduced himself and Salandra, and the farmer said he was Mariano.

"We were looking at the statues," Indy said. "Very interesting."

Mariano waved a hand as if they were of no importance. "There are many more near San Agustin. Hundreds. But we are not going that way."

"How long have you lived on the mountain?" Indy asked as they rode off.

"Seventy-eight years. I was born on the mountain. I have grown coffee all of my life."

Neither Indy nor Salandra had said anything about the Indian burial cave they'd passed through as they'd left the maze. Indy wondered what the old man knew about it. "Did you know there is a cave up there?"

"I don't go up there, not for many, many years. Ghosts live up there."

"I'm glad you didn't think that we were ghosts," Indy said.

Mariano laughed. "You two are foreign to me, and strange, but you are not ghosts. They never come out during the day. The sun burns their eyes."

"Have you seen these ghosts?" Salandra asked, curiously.

"Three times in my life I have heard their horrible cries. One time I came face to face with a ghost. I thought it was a man who was in need of help. I tried to carry him down the mountain, but he died and crumbled like he was made of old paper. I ran away, and when I came back with others, there was nothing left of him. From that day, I have never gone back up there."

What Mariano was saying sounded similar to Salandra's explanation of what happened to those who were venturing into the wrong world deprived of *nalca*. "I thought ghosts were already dead," Indy remarked.

"These ghosts were all dying. That's what it sounded like. These mountains are filled with memories of the ancient ones who lived here."

Hours passed. They drove by sugar cane plantations and descended into a peaceful valley shrouded in palms, bamboo, and agave. At sunset, the city came into view below them, a welcome sign beneath a sky that had faded to pink, orange, and pale green. "Popayan," Mariano announced.

The temperature was mild, which meant that the valley was a few thousand feet above sea level. They were soon passing bell towers, domes and church spires, plazas and fountains amid whitewashed stucco houses with colorful flowers blooming above patio walls. In the waning light, Indy thought he could be in Spain. When they finally reached the railroad station, they said farewell to the old farmer.

Indy hadn't told Salandra his plans yet, and he wasn't exactly sure what she had in mind. They walked into the open-sided station and Indy studied the schedule, which was posted on a tattered piece of paper next to the ticket window. To his dismay, he found that the train connected with Santa Marta on the Caribbean coast, rather than Cartagena. Now he'd probably have to take a boat to Cartagena before he could catch a ship going to the States.

He turned to Salandra, who was eyeing him curiously. "Um, I'm going to Santa Marta. You can come with me if you like," he said.

She smiled. "I'm glad you haven't forgotten me. Santa Marta is our destination. It's right where we want to go."

"It is?" He didn't like the sound of that. He reached into his boot and pulled out his money, then peered into the barred window. "When's the train leave for Santa Marta?"

"Ten minutes ago."

"We missed it?"

"No. It's late. It comes any time now."

Indy bought two tickets, and they moved out onto the platform.

"From Santa Marta, it's a five-day walk into the mountains to the Gatekeepers," Salandra explained. "The mountains are very close to the ocean. You'll see. It's a beautiful walk, too."

Indy was about to tell her he'd never wanted to go to her world in the first place, and he wasn't planning on going back. But at that moment a breeze sprang up, and a cloud of dust swirled around them on the platform. He shielded his face with his arm and backed away from the pesky dust devil.

"Are you okay?" Salandra looked as if the dust hadn't touched her.

"Salandra, I don't think . . ."

A whistle blew as the train chugged into the station, and his words were drowned out.

"What did you say?" she shouted.

He shook his head. "Nothing." He'd tell her when they were settled in their seats and on their way.

16

BREAKDOWN

September 1929
Santa Marta, Colombia

Salandra leaned her head against Indy's shoulder as the train chugged out of the station. Indy took her hand as he tried to think of a way to tell her his plans. But within seconds, she was sleeping. So much for that. He'd wait until morning, he told himself, and closed his eyes. His sleep was restless, and marred by a nightmarish train chasing him down the track. Then the engine transformed into the head of a monstrous snake and swallowed him. He was trapped inside it, and the interior of the train looked suspiciously like the maze. Then the huge frog-thing hovered inches in front of his face and repeated its message over and over: *You will spend eternity here unless you keep your promise. Eternity . . . Eternity.*

When the train rolled into Santa Marta at eight-thirty the next morning, Indy was more than ready to get off. But Salandra was still asleep. "Wake up. We're here." He was amazed that she could sleep so soundly. He'd been awake since the first light.

Her eyelids barely opened and she moaned softly. "I'm not feeling well. The *nalca*. Please."

Indy found the pouch nestled under Salandra's arm. She took a sip, then held up a hand. "Close the top."

"There's plenty here," Indy said. "Why don't you take more?"

"I'm saving it. You'll need it again when we go back."

"Yeah. There's been something I've been meaning to tell you about that. You know—"

The conductor loomed in front of them and asked to check their tickets. He briefly examined them, then moved on.

"Can you help me get up?" Salandra asked. "I feel weak."

He guided her into the aisle, but he didn't want to let the matter of their plans slip away again. "As I was saying. I just think that—"

"Ouch!" A huge suitcase slammed into his lower back. Indy glared at the double-chinned woman as she pushed past them. "*Señora*, you oughta get a horn for that thing."

Indy helped Salandra step down from the train. She seemed wobbly, and he steadied her. "You okay?"

Her nod was barely perceptible. She looked glassy-eyed, but Indy was determined to say what was on his mind. "About this trip. I was thinking that—"

"Are you from the States?"

Indy turned to see a kid, who looked about fourteen. His black hair was thick and unkempt. His skin was brown, and his dark eyes had a sparkle in them. "What's it to you?"

"I will be your guide," he said in heavily accented English. "I can show you the city and take you to see the hacienda of San Pedro Alejandrino. It's where Simón Bolívar died. I can give you a very good price for a tour."

Aggressive kid. "Not now."

Salandra's legs gave out, and she collapsed. Indy grabbed her around the waist. "I don't think we're going anywhere except to a hotel."

"Let me help," the kid said. He moved around to the other side of Salandra and draped her arm over his shoulder. But she was too tall for him to do any good.

"I'll handle the lady," Indy said. "Just lead us to a hotel."

"*Sí, señor*. My name is Ricardo. Please, follow me. I will get you a room, and a doctor to take care of the lady."

"No doctor," Salandra whispered.

"Just the room, Ricardo."

Indy and Salandra hobbled through the station and out to the street. Ricardo hailed a taxi, a vintage Model T, and they climbed aboard. It was a small village, but an ancient one, the first founded in the Americas. It had been an isolated outpost for the Spanish in the sixteenth century, and today, in 1929, it still seemed relatively isolated.

The main plaza was crisscrossed with walkways, and interspersed throughout the expanse were well-tended plots of flowers and shrubbery. A colonial ca-

thedral was situated on one side, and the hotel was
across from it. Indy thanked the driver, and out of
curiosity asked where he got spare parts when his taxi
broke down.

"From the other broken ones," he answered.

"Right this way," Ricardo said. "You will like it
here. The best hotel in Santa Marta."

Its dusky stone walls gave the hotel an ominous
look, but once they were inside, the morning sun
streamed through the high windows into the quaint
lobby of polished woodwork and colonial antiques,
creating a homey, comfortable feeling.

Salandra had recovered enough to walk on her
own, but as soon as they reached the second-floor
room, she eased onto one of the single beds. "Are you
going to be all right?" Indy asked.

"It's going to take me a couple of days to adjust to
your world."

My world, Indy thought. It sounded as if she was
conferring ownership on him. He didn't know what to
think of Salandra and her origin anymore. "I thought
you were a traveler. How come you're having so
much trouble?"

"I didn't have time to prepare for the change." Her
voice was soft, weak.

"How do you prepare?"

"Change of diet. Small quantities of *nalca* for several days. I don't remember ever feeling this sick. But
I'm not as sick as you were on the ship."

"How sick was that?"

"You were ill for more than two weeks. You almost
died."

The time factor again. He didn't think he'd ever
understand what had happened, and the last thing he

wanted to do was repeat the experience. He walked to the window and gazed over the plaza. "Salandra, listen. I've been trying to tell you that I'm not going back with you. I'm going home."

When there was no response, he turned. She was fast asleep again.

If ever there was a pirate's hangout, this place was it, Indy thought as he walked along the beachfront the next morning in search of a boat to Cartagena. Suspicious characters abounded, and he seemed to fit right in with his whip and fedora. No one paid him any heed.

My world, he thought, recalling Salandra's words. While she'd slept yesterday, he'd written a long letter to Brody, detailing what had happened to him. He'd probably be home before the letter got to Brody, but he'd wanted to write down his recollections while they were still fresh in his mind. Already, some memories were indistinct, blurred, shadowy, and he was confused about the sequence of events. He wasn't even sure how much of it had been a dream, and how much of it had actually happened.

Ricardo had been waiting in the hotel lobby, and accompanied Indy to the post office, then the telegram office where he wired Brody for money. Once Indy had made his plans for getting to Cartagena, he'd tell Salandra he was leaving as soon as the money arrived. She seemed much better this morning, but still hadn't been ready to leave the room.

A massive, craggy rock jutted out of the ocean a quarter mile offshore, and a small island was barely visible in the distance. Maybe someday this idyllic Caribbean coast, with its white sands and tranquil aqua waters, would attract throngs of foreign visitors. But the concept of tourism definitely hadn't arrived here yet.

Indy and Ricardo reached a harbor with a stone jetty. Several fishing boats were docked on a pier. Indy asked about a ride to Cartagena, but none of the fishermen was any help.

"Indy!" Ricardo called out as he hurried over to him. "I've found the captain of a freighter. It's not such a good boat, but he goes back and forth with supplies." He led Indy across a street and into a waterfront tavern. The place was dark, and it took a moment for their eyes to adjust. A crusty, bearded man, who looked as if he'd been drinking since sunrise, hovered over the bar, drink in hand.

"My friend here would like to go to Cartagena," the kid explained.

The bleary-eyed captain turned to Indy. "Come back in a week or so. I'll be ready to leave. But I'm going to need some money in advance."

"I'll think about it," Indy said.

"Don't think too long," the drunk called out after him.

"I'd be better off walking," Indy said to Ricardo as they left the tavern. He'd try again later.

"Señor Indy, I have a question," Ricardo asked as they headed back up the beach. "Why did you say that only you want to go to Cartagena? Is your lady friend staying here?"

"She's going hiking in the mountains when she's feeling better. I've got to go back to the States." Indy realized the comment probably sounded absurd, but he didn't care. The kid didn't know the circumstances and Indy wasn't about to explain.

"She's going up there alone?"

"She likes to hike," he said, lamely.

"Do you know where she is going?"

"Like I said, the mountains. The Sierra Nevada of Santa Marta."

"There are many peaks, but we call it one mountain. Its highest peak is almost nineteen thousand feet, and it's only twenty-six miles from the coast. That's closer to the ocean than any other mountain that big."

"Sounds like you know your facts."

"We studied the mountain in school, and the priest, Father James, used to take us on overnight trips up there."

"Are you still in school?"

"I had to quit to work. My family needs the money."

"What else do you know about the mountain?" Maybe he could hire Ricardo to guide Salandra. She'd probably need a guide.

Ricardo enthusiastically spilled a list of facts. He sounded as if he were practicing the fine art of tour guiding in a place with a conspicuous absence of people to guide. The coastal and lower slopes of the mountain were dry and arid, but a lush tropical forest grew in the moderate altitudes. Above that, a frigid, winter atmosphere prevailed on the high, wind-swept plains.

"Anyone live up there?"

"A few farmers, not many. The forest and slopes make it very difficult."

"Have you ever heard of any people on the mountain called the Gatekeepers?"

Ricardo frowned, then shook his head. "But maybe the Kogis know about them."

"Who?"

"The Kogis, you know, the Indians." He motioned with his hand. "They live way up high."

Indy had never heard of them, but he assumed they were a small tribe, possibly descendants of the Taironas, whose culture was known for its advanced gold-working techniques. They had flourished in the region until the arrival of the Spaniards. "Are they friendly?"

Ricardo hesitated. "The Kogis are not so friendly. Father James was always trying to talk to them about God. But they wouldn't listen to him. He said that of all the Indians, the Kogis are the most difficult to reach with religion. He said they were misguided souls, who had fallen into the hands of the devil."

Indy and Ricardo turned away from the beach and headed toward the plaza. Maybe he'd have a chat with the priest himself to see what else he could find out, Indy thought. He was starting to feel bad about his intentions to abandon Salandra. "Does Father James still go up the mountain to see the Kogis?"

Ricardo was quiet for a moment. "He went to visit them last month. He was expected back ten days ago, but nothing has been heard from him. The people are getting worried."

Indy mulled over what he'd heard. Now he was feeling guilty about abandoning a sick woman to an unknown fate. "I tell you what. If Salandra still wants to climb the mountain when she feels better, I'll go with her and see what we can find out about the priest."

"*Muy bien. Muy bien.* I will tell my mother, and she

will spread the word. Can I go, too? I can show you the way to the Indian village. I went there with the priest one time."

"We'll see." Indy's thoughts were already elsewhere. He'd accompany Salandra up the mountain, but that was all. Once she'd found her Gatekeepers, she was on her own.

17

THE SIERRA NEVADA

Indy sipped his coffee at the hotel restaurant and discreetly studied Salandra. Her recovery amazed him. Two days ago, he'd literally carried her to the room. Now she seemed not only well, but energetic.

"I gave Ricardo a list of supplies we'll need," she said. "He should have everything together in a couple of hours."

"Are you sure you've recovered enough?"

"Of course I have." She dismissed his concern and prodded him about Ricardo. "Did you tell him he could join us?"

"Not really." He took a bite of scrambled eggs. "I figured his mother wouldn't let him. Does he still want to go?"

She nodded. "I told him to get three horses. He can accompany us until we can't ride any further. After that we have to go on our own." She must have noticed the doubtful look in Indy's eyes, because she added: "Don't worry. I know the way. I've been down the mountain and back up many times."

Indy couldn't help but notice how she'd said down first, as if starting from the top of a mountain was the normal way to go. "By yourself?"

"Usually."

Somehow, he couldn't quite imagine her walking for days on the mountain, then showing up in this town. If she had managed to avoid trouble and survive the trek, she would have had her hands full here. She was tall and beautiful, a startling figure who attracted stares. But it wasn't the time to confront her about his doubts. Another matter was on his mind.

"There's something I haven't told you." Last night Salandra had still been groggy, and Indy had put off saying anything about the priest. But now he told her about the situation, emphasizing that hostile Indians might be involved. If he could discourage her from climbing the mountain, all the better. Maybe there was another way she could get back to her world.

"That's too bad about the priest, but I don't think that the Kogis were involved," she answered. "They don't care for missionaries. They're aloof, but they're not violent."

"Have you met any of them?"

She laughed. "You can't find the Gatekeepers without encountering the Kogis."

No matter how much Indy prodded her, she wouldn't say anything more about the Kogis or Gatekeepers. A few minutes later, they crossed the plaza to the hotel. The manager hailed Indy and told him that there was a wire for him from the States.

Great. His money had arrived. While Salandra waited for Ricardo, Indy headed to the telegraph office. A brief note from Brody accompanied the money. YOU'RE ALIVE! GREAT NEWS. HURRY BACK.

"I'm doing my best," Indy said under his breath, as he returned to the hotel.

He found Ricardo and Salandra waiting with the horses and supplies. Indy placed the money in a safe deposit box, and they left town by midmorning. They followed the shoreline for three or four miles along one of the most pristine stretches of beach Indy had ever seen. The deserted, white, sandy beach, the palm trees, and the tranquil, aqua Caribbean waters wove a seductive spell. He imagined swimming with Salandra, sharing the milk of the coconuts which littered the beach, and sleeping next to her under the stars. They'd send Ricardo on his way, and have the place to themselves.

They reached a secluded cove, and he couldn't stifle the urge any longer. Indy stopped his horse and climbed down. "Maybe we should spend a day here relaxing on the beach before we get started."

Salandra took in a deep breath and threw her head back. "It is nice here."

"I don't think you will like it so much, not after dark," Ricardo put in. "It's not a good place."

"Why not?" Indy asked. "It looks like a great place, if you ask me."

"You don't have any netting. The mosquitoes would keep you awake all night. And the vampire bats are even worse. You would be covered with blood by morning."

"Vampire bats?" Salandra said.

"Why didn't you tell us we needed nets?" Indy asked, suddenly disgruntled with their young guide.

"Because you didn't say you wanted to go camping

on the beach. If we keep going, we'll get high enough
today so that there will be no mosquitoes."

"And no vampire bats?" Salandra asked.

"None," he said.

"I think we should do what he says, Indy."

"Yeah. I guess so." Indy remounted his horse. "I
never liked beaches much, anyhow. Too much sand."

He prodded his horse, and they moved on, now
turning inland toward the foothills. In the distance,
two pale blue peaks glistened in the morning sun-
shine. They looked like diamonds suspended in the
sky.

They rode past almond and cashew nut trees, but
for the most part the coastal plain was covered by a
dry forest of thorny scrub brush and cactus and occa-
sional agaves and gourd trees. It was difficult to believe that they were within a few miles of a tropical
rain forest, and that the forest gave way to an icy
tundra.

The sun bore down on them, and Indy concentrated on a cooling image of himself swimming in the
soothing, blue waters. He imagined diving down to
the coral reef, past conch shells, sponges, and starfish.
He'd surface with a huge lobster in one hand and a
crab in the other, and Salandra, scantily clad, would
be gathering wood for a campfire. It wasn't going to
happen, but the image helped him pass the time.

By late afternoon, they had entered a humid tropical forest where the cedars and *tagua* palms shot up
more than a hundred feet above the forest floor. Beneath it grew a lush undergrowth of avocado and laurel, carob and rubber trees, as well as thorn bushes
and brambles laden with berries. Flowering liana
vines of several varieties added to the exuberant jun-

gle growth and held their parasitic grip on virtually
everything that grew. The ground was wet from a
recent downpour, and the water rushed down a
nearby stream. The temperature was moderate, a far
cry from the sultry coastal plain, and Indy was
pleased to find that Ricardo was right about the lack
of mosquitoes.

They dismounted, and walked the horses a ways
until they found a clearing near the stream for their
campsite. Indy could see why it would be easier to
walk than to ride from this point. They'd have to literally carve a trail for the horses.

Ricardo stayed in camp that night, and they ate a
thick stew prepared by the hotel's restaurant. As Indy
ate, he puzzled over the matter of the Kogis, the
priest, and the Gatekeepers. He knew that Salandra
didn't want him to even mention the Gatekeepers in
Ricardo's presence, and Indy certainly wasn't going to
discuss his plans to leave her on the mountain while
the kid was around.

He scraped the last spoonful from his wooden
bowl, then picked up the other two bowls and walked
over to the stream to wash them. Ricardo followed
him like a faithful dog. "Keep your eye out for
snakes," Indy said.

"I always do. Snakes and other things, too," Ricardo said, and he snatched something from Indy's
shoulder. Indy turned to see that Ricardo held a
seven-inch-long walking stick. The young guide
smiled. "It's harmless," he said, and he tossed it aside.

"What happened the time you went with the priest
to the Kogis' village?" Indy asked as they headed
back.

"Nothing much. I had to wait outside the village.

Father James was only there a short time. Then he came back and said that we would have to leave, that they wouldn't talk to him."

"And you just left?" Indy asked as they reached the camp.

Ricardo nodded. "No reason to stay."

Salandra was already lying in her hammock. She stared up toward the dark, starless sky shrouded by the thick forest canopy. He wondered what she was thinking. "You tired?"

"Where's Ricardo?" she asked in a low voice.

"Over by the horses."

"There's something about him that I can't figure out," she said.

"What do you mean?"

"I don't know, but I think he's hiding something from us."

Indy laughed. "Go to sleep. You're tired."

Indy hooked his hammock to a pair of trees a few feet from her. He thought again about what Ricardo had told him. It seemed odd to him that the priest would keep going back if the Kogis rejected him. After all, it was not exactly a short hike to the village. Maybe there was more going on than the kid knew, or was saying.

In the morning, Indy paid Ricardo for the supplies and his service, and added a generous tip. He thanked the kid and wished him well. Ricardo stuffed the money in his pocket without counting it. "Are you sure I can't come with you? I think it would be okay with my mother. I could leave the horses at the last farm we passed, and catch up with you."

"We'll do just fine from here, Ricardo. Don't worry. And we'll find out all we can about Father James."

"Thanks," Ricardo said sadly, and he watched Indy and Salandra move away into the verdant jungle.

The nearby screams of howler monkeys greeted them, and a flock of brightly colored parrots cavorted overhead. They followed animal trails, and at one turn surprised a couple of wild pigs that squealed as they ran into the forest. Salandra led the way, and seemed confident that they were moving in a southerly direction, away from the sea and toward the precipices. The forest formed a canopy high overhead, and the sunlight was further diffused by giant, dew-covered ferns that arched twenty feet above them.

By late morning, they came upon remnants of a stone trail. Indy brushed away a layer of moss and dirt to reveal flagstones neatly fitted next to one another. "There used to be a network of villages covering this mountain," he said, recalling what he knew of the region. "The Spaniards destroyed the civilization in a generation."

"I know," Salandra said. "Some of them escaped into the interior world."

With the help of the Gatekeepers, no doubt. "That sounds more like Indian myth than fact."

She smiled, but didn't say anything more.

The longer Indy was away from his experience in the interior world, the more dreamlike it became. But he decided he'd play along with her for awhile longer. "How many of these entrances between worlds are there?"

"There are many. I have access to several on three continents."

"Because you're the daughter of a king?"

"Not at all. Knowledge of the passage points is gained only through a determined effort. It is a quest of the highest dimension."

"I thought you said your council granted the privilege."

"Yes," Salandra answered. "But they have the power to protect only the primary gates, the ones that are most accessible."

"Which gates can Maleiwa pass through?"

"Too many."

"What about the one here on the mountain?"

"It's the easiest of all to enter. That's why it's guarded constantly."

For the next two days, Indy and Salandra continued climbing the Sierra. They waded across streams and rivers, and bathed in pools beneath waterfalls. The temperature was perfect, neither hot nor cold. But each afternoon, they had to find shelter for a couple of hours while torrential rains swept through the forest.

After the rain, which was always brief and left everything glistening, they plodded on through the soggy terrain. Only when they were following one of the ancient stone paths did their feet stay dry. On two occasions, Indy spotted human footprints along the trail, and wondered who else was treading these paths. Several times he paused to look around, certain that they were being watched, only to see a bird flit away or a snake slither into the underbrush.

By the third day, Indy's feet had developed several blisters. He was limping slightly, and slowing the pace. Late in the afternoon, as they followed a path bordered by an ancient stone wall shrouded in liana vines Salandra came to a sudden stop. A huge clay urn lay a few feet from the trail. Next to it was a freshly dug pit.

"*Huaqueros!*" Indy exclaimed. "They're looting the Tairona graves." He dropped into the pit and noticed several small bones scattered about, some a couple of inches under the loose soil. He was about to take a closer look at the bones, when Salandra called out to him.

She was staring into another pit several yards away. A human jawbone with teeth, and a couple of femur bones, poked through the dirt at the bottom. Next to the bones lay a shovel. "They're destroying everything here," Salandra said.

Indy scanned the forest. "They must still be around here."

As if on cue, three men, one with a shotgun, stepped out of the jungle. None of them was much more than five feet tall. All were thin and wearing tattered clothes covered with dirt. Their faces were grimy. "Who are you?" the one with the shotgun demanded.

"I was just about to ask you the same question," Indy said.

The men laughed. "You're after our gold, aren't you?" Shotgun said. "Well, we don't have any for you to steal."

"We're not looking for gold." Indy's hand was on his whip, and he was cautiously unhitching it. His body blocked their view of his hand.

Shotgun raised his weapon. "This is our discovery. Put your hands in the air," he ordered.

Indy did as he said. His whip hung loosely on his belt. But he wasn't about to take any chances. He figured they'd just found the ones who'd killed the priest.

"Get in the pit! Both of—*La mujer! Dónde está la mujer?*"

Indy glanced around and saw that Salandra was nowhere in sight. Two of the grave robbers darted around the clearing looking for her. Shotgun looked befuddled, and Indy took advantage of the confusion. He grabbed his whip and hurled it, snaring the barrel of the weapon. He jerked it out of the *huaquero's* grasp and scooped it up with his free hand.

The man cursed and rushed at Indy. They struggled for the gun and fell into the pit, where they rolled over one another. Ancient bones crushed beneath them. But Indy was bigger and stronger than his assailant, and he quickly overpowered him. He looked up, expecting to see the man's partners about to leap on him. But they were gone.

"Some friends you got, fellow. They took off."

The bone-chilling scream of a large cat ripped through the forest, and a few seconds later the two men raced back into the clearing. Their eyes were wide with terror; they leaped into the pit. But neither of them made any effort to assault Indy.

"Jaguar!" one of them shouted. "It's close."

"Don't move!" Indy turned the shotgun on the men. At the same time, he kept a wary eye on the jungle. "You guys scared of a little cat?"

"It was coming right for us," one of them said, still gasping for breath. "And it was huge."

Salandra emerged from the forest. "I see you've got everything under control," she said.

"Watch out!" Indy called. "There's a big cat out there."

"I think it's gone," she answered.

"Good. We've got our hands full right here." Indy jabbed the barrel of the shotgun at the gut of the *huaquero* who'd aimed it at him. "All right. What did you do with the priest?"

The man shook his head. "I don't know about no *padre.*"

"And I don't like your answer." Indy turned to the other two men. "Where is the priest?" He pointed the barrel between the eyes of the one who looked most frightened. "Who killed him?"

"*Señor,* we don't know nothing about no *padre.* We didn't kill anyone. We are hungry *campesinos.* We have families. We are not killers. We don't have no gold, either."

"It's the truth," one of the others said.

Indy turned back to the first man. "Why were you pointing the gun at me?"

"I thought you were a bandit."

"Let them go, Indy," Salandra said. "They're telling the truth."

It was exactly what he was thinking. But Indy wasn't quite ready to allow them to walk away. "Get your shovels, and get to work. You're going to put the dirt back."

When one of them protested, Indy swung the shotgun under his nose. "Something wrong?"

"No, *señor.*"

By the time the holes were filled, the sun was creeping into the forest, and shadows were lengthening. "Okay, get moving."

"Give the man his gun, Indy," Salandra said.

"Are you kidding?"

"They're not dangerous, and you can't take it to the interior. It won't go through the gate."

Indy broke open the shotgun and knocked out the cartridges. He flung them into the forest, then tossed the shotgun to its owner. "Don't let me catch you digging up any more graves. The next one will be your own."

The *huaqueros* turned and vanished into the forest. "I guess that's that," Indy said. "Except for one thing."

Once again, he was about to tell Salandra he wasn't going back to her world, but the words caught in his throat. Standing in a line on a ridge just above them were several men. Their black hair hung over their shoulders, and they wore baggy white tunics over calf-length pants. Each of them carried a net bag over his shoulder, and they held strange spindles in their hands.

"Salandra!"

"I see them."

"Kogis?"

"Yes . . . and the Gatekeepers. One and the same."

18

THE GATEKEEPERS

"Do you recognize any of them?" Indy asked in a quiet voice.

"Of course. I know all of them," Salandra replied. "They are my friends."

Indy waved; the Kogis stared down at him, but none returned his greeting. "I'm glad they're your friends. Why don't you ask them about the priest?"

"Not now." She took a couple of steps forward, and greeted the Kogis in a guttural language. Then she shifted to Spanish. "Mama Juan. We are on our way to the gate. Are you going our way?"

The Kogi who appeared to be the eldest of the group turned to the man next to him, and whispered a few words. Indy moved next to Salandra. "What did you call him?"

Before she answered, the old Kogi who had spoken motioned impatiently with his hand for them to climb the slope. Indy was wary, but Salandra seemed at ease.

"Mama Juan, I want you to meet my friend, Indy. He's going back with me. We need his help."

The man she addressed stood barely five feet tall. His face was a rete of wrinkles. He studied Indy as if he were a great curiosity. "So you are the one. I've heard about you."

"You have?"

Then Mama Juan pointed toward the jungle. "This way. Come with us."

As the Kogis moved off, Indy took Salandra by the arm. Indy was curious about the Kogis, but he was not going to be dragged back to Salandra's world. "I'm going back to Santa Marta."

She glanced toward the Kogis, then to Indy. "Please come with me. At least tonight. In the morning, if you feel the same way, we'll say good-bye to each other."

Indy was tempted to walk away and not look back. But he still didn't have an answer to the matter about the priest, and he'd promised Ricardo he'd find out. He nodded, and they hurried after the Kogis in the growing dusk. Tonight, he told himself, he'd find out what had happened to Father James, and tomorrow he'd begin his descent.

They moved quickly through the forest. Indy's blistered feet ached with every step. If the Kogis were following a path, Indy couldn't see it. They were moving so fast, and the light on the forest floor was so dim, that everything was a deep green blur.

It was nearly dark when they reached another clearing in which stood a single round house with a steeply sloping thatched roof. It was capped with a second smaller roof from which projected a wooden stake like a radio antenna, and on the stake were several round, flat disks of various sizes. There was a wide doorway, but no door, and the walls were made of a latticework which would allow easy access to insects as large as sparrows. At least it would keep out the rain, he thought.

"Their village?" Indy asked.

"No, just a stopping place for the night," Salandra answered, as the Kogis filed inside. "Let's wait out here until they invite us in."

Salandra hadn't said much about the Kogis, and she'd intentionally omitted the fact that they were the Gatekeepers. But now that he thought about it, he should've figured that out from what Ricardo had said about the priest's encounters. If the Kogis had told him about the interior world, the priest would definitely think that they were in cahoots with the devil.

"When are you going to ask them about the priest?" he asked, as he sat down on a rock and loosened his boots.

"After we've eaten."

Indy pulled off one of the boots and rubbed his foot. "Dinner first. Always a good idea. What's the story with your friend's name?" He loosened his other boot. "Why is he a mama?"

She laughed. "The *mama*s are the priests." She knelt down and pulled off the boot and his sock. "Their god is feminine, the earth goddess, but only men are *mama*s."

"I get it. I think." He watched in fascination as Salandra ran a hand over the bottom of his foot, but never touched it. He felt a warm, tingling sensation, and wasn't sure whether it was from her hand, or just the foot reacting to being out of the boot.

"They compare the Mother Goddess to the Sierra Nevada, from its snowy peaks to the ocean," she added. "The forest is her skin; the rivers are her veins. The night sky is her blanket. They see it as both symbolic and true."

Indy looked up to the twinkling stars, the first he'd seen since they'd entered the rain forest. "A nice analogy," he commented. "Is that the same Mother Goddess you mentioned?"

"In a way, yes. We call her Rhea."

"So did the ancient Greeks."

"It's no coincidence," she said matter-of-factly. "This world in many ways is a reflection of the interior world, and vice versa. How's your foot feel?"

"Much better. What are you doing?"

"Healing your blisters." She moved to the other foot, and he immediately felt the warm, tingling sensation again. This time he was sure that it was somehow related to what she was doing.

He was just starting to relax, when he saw a long, slender, brightly striped snake sidling through the clearing toward them. "Don't move!"

Salandra peered at the snake as Indy reached for his whip. It wasn't huge, but it looked like a coral snake. Poisonous and deadly. It stopped a few feet from them, raised its head, and seemed to peer at Salandra. Then it sidled off, heading toward the jungle, and Indy's hand eased off his whip.

"Snakes are a good sign," Salandra said.

"Snakes are never a good sign, as far as I'm concerned," Indy said, as the creature slithered out of sight. But they were symbolic of wisdom and the earth in some American Indian lore. Another reflection of worlds, he thought.

The night creatures were tuning up for their nonstop concert, which would last until dawn. The jungle might be the Mother Goddess, but he was looking forward to hitching his hammock inside the house, even if it wasn't exactly bug-free or snake-proof. Then he wondered if they would be safe from the Kogis. "What if they did kill the priest? Don't you think they could just as well turn against us?"

"No, I don't," she said, patting his foot as she finished her healing. "They know me, and they like you."

"What makes you think they like me?"

"They watched how you dealt with the *huaqueros*. You impressed them."

"How do you know they were watching?"

"I saw them when I slipped away into the forest."

Indy recalled something he'd almost forgotten about. "Did you see that jaguar?"

"That was Mama Juan."

"Oh, yeah?" Indy was incredulous. "I suppose you saw him turn into a jaguar."

"No, but it's still true."

"But how do you know it was him?"

She laughed and shook her head. "I've never known a man who asks as many questions as you do. Besides, I've done it myself."

"You've turned into a jaguar?"

"Not a jaguar. A falcon."

"Is that how you get down the mountain when you come here?"

She nodded. "And I usually appear in Santa Marta as an older woman, so I don't attract attention."

He recalled her saying something about Pincoyans changing shapes, but everything about that place seemed unreal to him. "Are you saying that you can just change shape to be whatever you want to be?"

"I've told you that I'm a sorcerer, a witch."

"Then why didn't you just fly up the mountain, rather than take the tedious way?"

She smiled and touched his hand. "Because you came along."

Well, he wasn't going to be around for long. "Why don't you change into something now?" he challenged. "I'd like to see that for myself."

Salandra pulled her hand away. Her face seemed to shift. Her eyes became larger, her head rotated to the side, and she blinked. For a moment, Indy thought he was looking at the face of a falcon. Then she looked at him again and he saw nothing had changed. A momentary illusion. "I don't perform tricks, Indy. Reshaping is an act of power which is done with purpose, not for exhibition."

Mama Juan stepped outside and motioned for them to come into the house. As they moved toward the doorway, Indy wondered if the interior world was a reflection of her sorcery, and he'd been caught inside the reflection.

The men were seated about the floor of the hut, and as Indy and Salandra found places among them, the food was served. No one spoke to either of them during the meal. It was almost as if they were not there.

Dinner consisted of a mix of corn and yucca and other vegetables Indy didn't recognize, all of which had been wrapped in banana leaves and baked over a fire. Unless someone had been here preparing the

meal, the food must have been precooked, because it
had only been on the coals for a few minutes. The
meal was delicious, and was served with cups of tea
sweetened with honey.

When the Kogis finished eating, the men again busied themselves with their spindles, apparently spinning thread from a raw fiber. The spindles were
shaped like tops, thick in the center and tapering toward either end where a central shaft protruded. "Are
they weavers?"

"Yes, and much more," Salandra said.

Indy looked up to see Mama Juan sitting down
across from him. His skin was the color and texture of
leather that had been left out in the rain and dried. It
looked as if it would crack if he changed his expression. But to Indy's surprise the network of fine wrinkles shifted into a broad smile as the old man held up
a spindle. Indy nodded, uncertain what was so fascinating about it. This one, unlike the others, didn't
even have any fiber around it. It consisted of a foot-
long shaft which pierced the centers of several
wooden disks. The largest of the disks was located in
the center, and the ones above and below were pro-
gressively smaller. Indy counted nine of them in all.

"This is all that is," the old Indian said.

Indy stared at the spindle, uncertain what to say.

Mama Juan tapped the central disk. "This is the
plane on which we live. It is called *Ninulanc.*" He ran
his fingers over the upper disks. "These are the
higher planes, *Mamanulang, Mulkuakukui, Nyuinu-
lang,* and *Xatsalnulang.*" Then he moved his finger to
the disks on the lower side. "These are the realms of
the underworld, *Haba Sivalulang, Haba Kanenulang,
Haba Kaneexan, Haba Guxanexan.*"

He went on to explain that the Kogi houses were built in the same shape as the top half of the spindle. The floor was *Ninulanc,* and the underworld was an abstract extension of the house, existing below the earth. "The daytime sun weaves in white thread, from west to east, while its nighttime counterpart travels in the underworld from west to east, weaving a black thread in the fabric of time."

The analogy fascinated him, but Indy wondered if they were all madmen cut off from the world, existing in their own reality, one in which spindles had assumed far greater meaning than they deserved. He watched Mama Juan closely as the old man pointed at the center point of the large spindle. "The Kogis are here at the gate to the underworld. We are the guardians. We work our spindles day after day to make sure that the weave of the universe, above and below, stays together as a finely woven piece of fabric."

"That sounds like a lot of work," Indy said, recalling that Salandra had said she did the same sort of thing.

"It is the job of the Elder Brothers." Mama Juan set aside the empty spindle, and picked up another one bulging with thread. Attached to the thread was a primitive-looking loom, which consisted of four poles slashed together in the shape of a square. Mama Juan pulled the wooden shuttle across the loom. He was making a piece of cloth.

"I thought you were the Gatekeepers."

"We are many things, but we are first the Elder Brothers. He pointed at Indy. "You, Younger Brother, have your toys, your trains and your airplanes, but you and those of your kind are like thoughtless children. You are endangering the fabric." He tapped the cloth extending from the loom, then turned to Salandra. "The same is true for you. Your people possess the toys of the mind, but you too are heedless of the delicate weave of the fabric. Too many of you pass to this side with ill intent."

"Mama Juan," Salandra protested. "It is not all of us. Indy and I want to do what we can to help maintain the balance between the exterior and interior. We are especially concerned about Maleiwa, the Wayua. He is a great threat to the balance, or as you say, the fabric."

"There's a priest missing, too," Indy blurted. "Father James. I think you know him."

Mama Juan's dark eyes bore into Indy. "You're an impatient man. You don't want to hear about the duties of the Gatekeepers because you don't believe. You are more interested in our ancestors. You think we are crazy Indians left behind by time. You don't realize the importance of what we do here."

Indy was getting fed up with the lecture. Sure, there were problems in the world, but he didn't like being the symbol of all that was bad. "I was asked to find out about the missing priest," he repeated.

"There is no missing priest." Mama Juan raised his head and gazed over the other men. He nodded, and someone sitting in the shadows on the far side of the group stood up and walked along the wall. He was a slight figure, even among the Kogis, and unlike the others, his hair was short. As he neared them, Indy recognized the face in the flickering light.

It was Ricardo, dressed in Kogi garb.

"What are *you* doing here?" Indy asked. In spite of his short hair, Ricardo did vaguely resemble the other Kogis.

The boy smiled, and sat down between Indy and Salandra. "I've been waiting for you. I prepared the meal. Did you like it?"

Indy ignored the question. "So you're a Kogi?"

"No." He nodded toward Salandra. "I'm from her world, from Pincoya. I told the Gatekeepers you were on your way, and asked them to meet you."

Salandra's face was frozen in a look of shock. She seemed genuinely startled by Ricardo's revelation. "You didn't know?" Indy asked.

She shook her head ever so slightly.

"I had to block you," Ricardo said. "If you found out, you would've told him, and he would've left."

"You made up the story about the priest?" Salandra asked.

Ricardo smiled impishly. "Indy needed a push. I wanted to make sure he came with you."

"Yeah, well, I've got news for both of you." Indy stood up. "I'm going home. I'm not taking another step up this mountain."

He didn't know where he was going tonight, but he didn't want to stay here. Not another minute.

Salandra leaped up. "Indy, I need you. We all need your help. You are the only one who can—"

Indy spun around. "I don't believe that story," he snapped. "Let Ricardo get it. He's clever."

He didn't think that she had been involved with Ricardo and his tricks, but it didn't matter. "Salandra, I enjoy a good adventure, but I've got my limits. And your world, whatever it is, is definitely across my border."

"I understand." Her voice was barely a whisper.

Indy turned to thank the old Indian for the dinner, but Mama Juan was paying him no heed. He was busy making his piece of cloth. Indy glanced at Ricardo. "Nice try, kid."

Indy moved outside, and Salandra followed. He jammed his hands into the pockets of his leather jacket. He was ready to leave, and he didn't know what more to say to her. "That's real swell, that the men help the women with the weaving."

"The Kogi women don't weave."

"They don't?"

"The Kogis are a reflection of the symbols that guide them. The earth is female and passive. That's why the women tend the gardens. The shuttle is the active part of the weaving process, and it's male. So only the men weave."

"Swell," he said again. He slung his pack, with the hammock and food in it, over his shoulder. "Salandra, I've got to go. Don't try to stop me."

"Do you know why you went to Chiloé, instead of staying on Easter Island?"

"At this point, it doesn't matter."

She gazed up toward the sky. "I think it does. It's because we are linked like stars in a constellation."

"Yeah? I think you've been around these Kogis too long. You're starting to sound like them."

"Please, before you go, listen to what I have to say. We are counterparts, you and I. That's what those statues, the double, are about."

He shook his head. "You lost me."

"Each of us has a counterpart in the other world. We are reflections of each other, even though we don't look alike or even act alike."

Now he'd really heard everything. "If we don't look alike or act alike, what makes us counterparts?"

"Our spirit. We have the same spirit."

Indy found something touching in what she said. Her philosophy was as quaint and unusual as the Kogis. He reached out, took her hand, and started to kiss it. Instead, he pulled her to him. Their lips met. But at that moment, two men rushed out of the forest, racing past them and into the house.

Indy jerked his head back. "Who was that?"

"Listen!" Salandra hissed.

A jabber of voices. "What is it? Can you understand them?"

She listened a moment longer, then nodded. "They're coming. We've got to go. Come with me, hurry!"

"Who's coming?"

"Maleiwa and his men. They've breached the gate. They're on the mountain."

She tugged once on his arm, then let go and dashed toward the house as the men poured out. She glanced back to where he stood in the darkness, and motioned him to join her. But he didn't move.

"Indy!"

"No!" he yelled. "I'm not going any further." He strode away in the opposite direction, proving to himself that he could break the spell that Salandra seemed to hold over him. When he reached the edge of the clearing, he paused, remembering the snake had gone this way. But there was no sign of it. Impulsively, he glanced back.

Salandra and the Kogis had already vanished into the forest. Indy stood there a moment, wondering if he'd made a mistake. *Too late now.* He plunged into the forest. The further he could get tonight, the bet-

ter. He'd walk until dawn, then rest for a few hours.
The sooner he got off the mountain, the happier he'd
be. He wanted nothing more to do with Kogis or
Wayua, Maleiwa or Salandra. It was over for him. It
was definitely over.

19

INTO THE INTERIOR

Salandra raced into the night with the Kogis. The Indians moved swiftly along the trails, and eventually blended into the forest. She stopped, uncertain which way to go. Maleiwa's warriors were nearby. She sensed it in every pore of her body.

The Kogis couldn't stop Maleiwa once he'd crossed through the gate, and now the Gatekeepers were scattering across the mountain, heading for secret hiding places as their ancestors had done centuries ago, when the conquistadors had driven them from their villages.

She wondered if she should have stayed with Indy. But she'd panicked and run when he refused to go with her. She should go back and find him. She was certain that Maleiwa was here because he had realized that Indy was on the mountain, and heading for the gate. That was the only explanation that made sense to her. He was here to kill Indy, the only person in either world who could disrupt his plans.

The two men who had rushed to the house with the news had been among those guarding the gate when Maleiwa's forces arrived. As they'd entered the clearing, they'd cried out that Maleiwa carried a magical weapon that allowed him to breach the gate. She had no doubt they were talking about the unicorn's horn.

She heard a thrashing sound a short distance away. She turned to flee, but voices surrounded her. The forest was alive with Maleiwa's men, and there was no time to escape, nowhere to go. She closed her eyes, squatted down and concentrated. She said a few words under her breath. She felt the familiar dizzying sensation brought on by transformation. Then, for several seconds, she was unaware of anything.

A falcon flapped its wings and flew for cover in the forest canopy. A moment later, several tall men armed with dart guns strode across the very place where Salandra had stopped on the trail.

A few minutes earlier, Indy had wanted nothing more than to get out of here. Now, as he headed through the dark forest, he suddenly felt a sense of uncertainty. He was free to leave, and no one was around to try to stop him. Yet, he regretted the way he'd left Salandra. Not that he hadn't warned her.

No, he told himself. He'd made the right decision to strike out on his own, to head home. Besides, her last-ditch ploy to change his mind had been ridiculous. Pathetic, he told himself. She'd tried to make it seem as if they were sort of like brother and sister, or even closer. Had she really thought that would make him go with her? Now he wondered if even the supposed arrival of Maleiwa and his troops might have been another ruse to keep him from leaving. If there was an army on the mountain, he certainly wasn't aware of it. Maybe Ricardo had dreamed it up. Strange kid.

Don't think about it, none of it, Indy told himself. He stumbled over a root. Maybe he should just set up his hammock somewhere and go to sleep. Why should he walk all night? He'd sleep and forget about everything. Salandra. Maleiwa. Ricardo. Mama Juan. All of them.

A branch snapped to his right, nearby. He paused. Listened. Footsteps. Someone was hurrying along the same animal trail. The forest was thick around him, leaving just one way to go. He hurried down the trail. After a couple of minutes, he stopped to catch his breath. Now he didn't hear anything. He started ahead again, but stopped short when someone stepped out of the trees, blocking his way. Ricardo.

"You trying to scare me, kid? What are you doing here?"

"Hi, Indy. I don't want you to lose your way."

"Don't worry about it. I've found my way this far, and I figure I can make it down this mountain the same way I made it up. By my own two feet."

"But, Indy, you're going the wrong way. You've got to help us stop Maleiwa." Ricardo was pleading with him now.

"What's your story, anyhow?"

"My father was killed because he opposed Maleiwa when his troops arrived in Pincoya. My mother and I were going into hiding when we were caught. I got away, but I don't know what happened to her." His voice trailed off. "I found my way to the gate, and the Kogis took me in."

"Don't you need *nalca*?"

"Of course, and I have to go back soon. Will you come with me?"

"It's not my battle, Ricardo."

"It's everyone's battle, Indy. Everyone who can help, and you can help more than anyone. Many people from my world know what's going on, and some of us know about you, too. Some think you're a myth. They even think your world is a myth." He grinned, his white teeth lining up in his mouth like a freshly painted picket fence. "But I know you're real."

The sharp call of a bird cut through the quiet. Indy glanced up, glimpsed wings and a beak, and ducked. Feathers fluttered against his hair. "I thought birds were supposed to sleep at night," he muttered.

"An omen," Ricardo said.

"No, just a bird," Indy responded.

The sound of voices silenced him. He and Ricardo backed into a thicket of ferns seconds before a dozen men, armed with crossbows like the ones Indy had seen in Pincoya, strode down the trail, passing within several feet of them.

"What are they doing here?" Indy whispered. "I thought Maleiwa wanted to make a deal with Hitler. He lives on another continent."

"They're looking for you," Ricardo said.

"Me!"

"Shh!"

Someone else was moving down the trail. Indy tensed. Whoever it was had stopped. Ferns rustled. Belatedly, he reached for his whip, and then he saw

Mama Juan's face. The old Kogi priest motioned for them to come out.

"There are hundreds of Wayua on the mountain. They know you are here. You must come with me. Quickly. Or they will find you."

"Swell." Indy wasn't sure he wanted to follow the Kogi anywhere. But he didn't like the idea of getting caught by Maleiwa's men. "Okay. Lead the way."

They charged through the forest, and once again Indy lost all sense of place. He kept his eyes on Mama Juan's white cotton tunic and forgot about everything. His blistered feet felt surprisingly better after Salandra's ministrations, but he still had a difficult time keeping up with the elderly Kogi. While Indy thrashed against the underbrush, Mama Juan seemed to glide through it. Every so often Indy heard a sound behind him, and knew that Ricardo was keeping up with them. If Maleiwa's men were all over the mountain, Mama Juan was somehow finessing a route that missed all of them.

Indy lost track of time as well as place. Mama Juan's tunic had turned into a dove gracefully flapping its wings, and Indy's strides became longer and longer and the thicket seemed to bend out of his way. It was as if they were part of a current which flowed through the forest. He was not only picking up speed; he was no longer gasping for breath. He'd gotten a second wind, but it was more than that. It was as if he had a second body he'd never known about.

Suddenly, a huge ceiba tree seemed to appear out of nowhere. It stood out, luminous against the night, separate from the forest. They were rushing toward it, and it was as if there were no other trees around them. Indy wanted to stop and gaze at the tree, but before he could slow down, the dove that was Mama Juan flew right into it and vanished. Indy tried to stop, but instead he was catapulted toward the tree. At the last second he saw a gaping hole in the trunk and realized that the Kogi must have ducked into it.

He dropped to his hands and knees, crawled into the opening, and immediately tumbled down a slope of gnarled roots. A shelter of some sort, hollowed out inside the tree, he thought. A great hiding place. But when he looked up, he saw he was not inside the tree at all. A hole opened up in front of him. The same hole in the same trunk of the same luminous tree. It had to be some sort of optical illusion. He was sure that he had already entered the tree.

Indy called out to Mama Juan. There was no answer, and where was Ricardo? He tried to look around, but couldn't take his eyes from the hole in the trunk. He didn't know what else to do but crawl into the hole again. This time, though, the floor was flat, and felt like compacted earth and rock. Indy kept crawling, afraid that if he looked up, he would find another illusion.

Finally, he decided to see where he was. The darkness had been replaced by a pale gray light. Yet it was too early for dawn. He wasn't in the tree. In fact, there wasn't a single tree in sight. He stood up and felt a cool wind, as he stared out over a vast rocky, desolate plateau. Not far from him the land abruptly ended.

"Hey! There you are!" Indy spotted Mama Juan standing by a mound of rocks near the edge of the plateau. He waved, but the Kogi priest wasn't looking his way. Indy hurried ahead, and as he neared Mama Juan he glimpsed several floating islands. No, not islands, but mesas or buttes that rose high above a grassy plain hundreds of feet below them.

"Where are we, anyhow?"

Mama Juan turned and peered at him, but said nothing. Indy already knew the answer. The mesas in the distance were tilted, curving upward toward the silver sky. He was back in the interior world, right where he didn't want to be, and he was feeling heavy and drowsy.

"Roraima. We are on top of a *tepui*." It wasn't Mama Juan who had spoken, but a man who had been standing out of sight by the rocks. He was tall, broad-shouldered, and bearded. He had peculiar green eyes that were somehow familiar.

"Who are you?"

"I am Vicard."

"Do I know you?"

"You know me as—"

Indy staggered a couple of steps. The interior world was pressing in upon him. He felt as if he was about to be crushed, about to melt into a puddle. It was happening all over again. Whatever else Vicard said, Indy heard none of it. He tottered and collapsed.

Hours had passed since Maleiwa's men had started scouring the mountain. Salandra, still in the shape of a falcon, was perched on the spindle that protruded through the top of a Kogi temple, the largest of the buildings in the village. Cone-shaped roofs of the other houses surrounded her, but the village was quiet, and it wasn't because the Kogis were asleep. They'd all fled when the Wayua warriors had poured through the gate.

Now, peering through a small opening at the base

of the spindle, she watched the tall, bald man as he paced in front of his chiefs, who had assembled to report to their leader. Maleiwa was draped in the traditional Wayua tunic that ended at midthigh and was tied at his waist with a wide cloth belt. She knew that when, and if, he met Hitler, Maleiwa would wear not only different clothing, but a different face, one which would appeal to Hitler's image of the superior man.

Maleiwa was not a shape shifter like herself, but an adept illusion shaper, who could appear to others as he wished without making an actual transformation. No doubt his skin would be pale and he would be as blond as Beitelheimer, whom Hitler had mistakenly believed to be a man of the interior world. But Beitelheimer had abandoned his mission, and now the Wayua leader had to act quickly or he would lose the confidence of his potential ally.

As Maleiwa spoke, she anxiously listened to every word. "Call the men back," he said. "They won't find him. He's not on the mountain."

"Are you certain?" one of his chiefs asked.

"Of course I am. I can feel that he is gone, and I know where he went. He's back in our world. That's the only place he could have gone. Otherwise, I would know he is here. But we'll find him."

Had Indy really gone back? Salandra wondered. She'd searched the mountain, but found no trace of him. She had to trust Maleiwa's second sight. It was not only strongly developed, but she was sure that the unicorn's horn was helping him to detect Indy's whereabouts.

The falcon soared from the top of the temple and flew higher up the mountain. It was finally dawn, and the outline of the snowy peaks stood out clearly against the pale blue morning sky. She flew over alder and myrtle and laurel and innumerable varieties of wild flowers. It was cooler here, almost too cold for a falcon. But she wouldn't be here for long, nor would she remain a falcon.

She circled over a rocky ledge, and spotted the dark opening. Nearby, several Wayua warriors guarded the entrance. One of them looked up and pointed at the falcon as it swept down and grazed their heads. They ducked, then aimed their weapons, firing darts wildly, but Salandra was already past them and winging through the dark cave toward a distant circle of light.

She emerged in a vast grassland where the familiar *tepui*s of Roraima jutted hundreds of feet into the air. Some of them were dry and rocky, while others were covered with jungle and inhabited by strange creatures. But Roraima was known for its wild and deadly beasts. That was why the population lived in protected areas within the *tepui*s. Yet, they felt neither trapped nor frightened by their surroundings. Roraimans could usually sense trouble before it arrived, and they knew how to avoid it when journeying outside of their *tepui*s.

Salandra flew low over the *tepui*, itself known as Roraima, that housed the largest city in the region. An area atop the massive *tepui* was a garden, and she could see dozens of Roraimans strolling along the paths. If they were concerned about Maleiwa's takeover of Pincoya, none of them showed any sign of it.

The Roraimans were physically notable for their long ears, which extended two or three inches longer than those of their short-eared Wayua neighbors. The

Roraimans were the first to inhabit the exterior world, and their heritage was still visible in the *moais* of Easter Island.

The Roraimans dressed in a similar fashion to the Kogis, wearing baggy white pants and long tunics, except they also wore rounded, white hats with a short rim all the way around. The first time she had seen a bowler in the exterior world, she had stopped and stared in fascination. Except for their color, and the fact that in the exterior they were worn only by men, they were almost identical to the Roraiman headgear.

She landed in a tree on the *tepui* and tried to feel Indy's presence. Instead, she immediately sensed Wayua guards. So they were here, quietly watching, and controlling. She spotted a pair of the robed guards with their crossbows. Then she saw several Roraimans gathered near a fountain, and she flew to another tree. They were discussing the situation with the Wayua.

"They will make Roraima safe for us," said a woman who was about Salandra's age. "They will destroy the wild beasts once and for all, and we can live peacefully outside of the *tepuis*."

"We can never live in peace as long the Wayua control us," a young man countered. "We've got to stop them, and the sooner the better."

Suddenly, a dart struck the man in the back, and the Wayua guards she'd seen rushed forward and dragged him away. So that was how it was, she thought.

She scanned again for Indy, just to make sure she had not missed him. But then she picked up something else. A signal meant only for her. Vicard!

He wasn't here, but he wasn't far away. The falcon took wing again, its heart pounding. Salandra shifted directions when she felt the pull weakening. Then it grew stronger and stronger, and she soared with the wind. She lost track of time and distance. Finally, she circled a barren *tepui*. She was far from the center of Roraima, actually very near Wayua. Then she saw him, waiting.

She landed a short distance away. The falcon flapped its wings for the last time as a whirlwind swirled around it. The bird vanished from sight, and when the whirlwind dissipated, Salandra was squatting on the ground, her face pressed against her knees. Slowly, she unfolded herself, stood up, then smiled broadly and raced toward the tall bearded man.

King Vicard. Her father.

20

ON THE *TEPUI*

The voice came out of a dream. Salandra stood in front of him, an illusion wearing a gauzelike gown that bunched around her ankles. The wind blew through her copper hair, which brushed against her cheeks. Her emerald eyes shone brightly, and her mouth was turned up in a smile.

"Indy, wake up . . . wake up."

Her image blurred, then came back into focus. "But you'll disappear."

She laughed. "You're half asleep, but you can wake up all the way now."

Slowly, he pushed up on his elbows. Salandra was here, and so was the bearded man, Vicard, tapping a finger against his chin. Indy looked around and tried to take in everything at once. He was in a room with stone walls, lying on a pile of blankets. But the room was roofless; it looked out onto the silver sky.

He closed his eyes, opened them again. It was still

the same. "Salandra . . . what are . . . you doing
here . . . and where . . . are we?" His tongue was
thick; his words slurred.

"You're in Roraima. Here, take this. It'll help you."
She passed him a cup.

He looked into it and saw a thick, yellowish liquid.
"*Nalca?*"

She nodded. "You need some more."

He sipped it, and made a face. "How long have I
been here?"

"More than a week."

"But it seems like I just got here. I felt a little dizzy
and passed out."

"That you did," Vicard said, "but it's as Salandra
says. We've been here eight days."

Indy shook his head. How could he have lost all
that time? He stood up, and held onto the wall to
balance himself. But his dizziness was only momentary. "Who are you, anyhow?"

"I'm Vicard, as I told you before. King of Pincoya."

"My father, Indy," Salandra said.

Vicard gripped his forearm, and Indy's hand fell
across the king's forearm. A Pincoyan handshake, no
doubt.

"Nice to meet you. I think." He looked out of the
hut onto a rocky plateau. "This is Roraima?"

"Only a small and remote part of it," Salandra said.

"We're on the same *tepui* where you and I entered
with Mama Juan," Vicard said.

"I don't remember coming here with you," Indy
muttered.

"Indy, he was Ricardo," Salandra said. "He took
the shape for protection."

Just what he needed to hear. "Don't tell me any

more. I don't want to hear it." Indy walked outside the hut, and Salandra followed him. Desolation surrounded them. Several buttes tilted in the distance, their bases seemingly climbing the sky. "I don't get it. If this is Roraima, where are the people? Where do they live?"

She told him.

He rubbed his neck. "You mean we're on the roof of one of the cities?"

"No, not this one," she said. "Most of them are just what they seem. Buttes, as you call them. We're well hidden here. There's not much chance that we'll be found. But we can't stay here, either."

The *nalca* was already taking effect. Indy's dizziness was disappearing, and he felt energetic. "Fine with me. I'm ready to go back." He spotted a pool of water a short distance away. He realized how thirsty he was. "Can I drink it?"

"Of course," Salandra answered. "It's our water source."

A stream led away from the pool and wound toward the edge of the *tepui*. The water was literally bubbling to the surface of the pool, probably from a spring inside the *tepui*. He dropped to one knee, cupped a handful of water, and sipped. It was sweet, and tasted pure. He leaned down and drank deeply until his thirst was quenched.

As he and Salandra returned to the hut, Indy noticed a faraway look on Vicard's face, and wondered if he was thinking of his lost kingdom. The look was neither sorrowful nor hopeful, but one of resigned acceptance.

"So where's Mama Juan?" Indy asked Vicard, who had snapped out of his reverie.

"He went back," the king responded. "He only delivered you here."

"That strange tree," Indy said, recalling what had happened. He turned to Salandra. "Did you come here that way, too?"

She shook her head. "I went through the main gate. It leads directly to Roraima, the main city."

Like Pincoya, the city and the region had the same names, he thought. "They weren't trying to catch you?"

"Oh, yes," she replied. "But they couldn't stop me. I flew through the gate, then over the city, and then here when I got Vicard's message."

"You flew," he repeated. Then he recalled the falcon story she'd told him.

She nodded. "Maleiwa knows you're hiding here somewhere. It's taken a great effort to block him from finding you."

"What if I leave?"

"We can't block him at the gates. It's impossible. He would find you immediately."

There always seemed to be a catch when it came to going home. "So I can't go back right now. What are we eating here, rocks?"

"We have a cache of food," Vicard said. "We've been waiting for you to recover from the transition."

"What about the tree? Can't I go back through it?" he asked.

"That was Mama Juan's entrance," Salandra said. "We don't have access to it. Besides, we've got to go to Wayua right away."

"Hold on. That's Maleiwa's home base, isn't it?"

"Exactly," Vicard said. "You've got to go there and get the alicorn from him."

"So it's back to that again."

"Listen to me, Jones." Vicard's voice was stern. "As long as you are alive, Maleiwa will be after you. If you return to your life, he will hunt you. As long as he has the alicorn, we cannot stop him from entering the exterior world. Now what are you going to do?"

Indy had heard enough. "All right. All right. Let's go and get this over with one way or another."

Vicard clasped him on the shoulder. "Nothing you do for the rest of your life will be as important as what you are about to do."

That was especially true if he didn't survive, Indy thought.

A few minutes later, the three of them were on their way. They crossed the plateau, leaning into the wind until they reached the edge. They followed a narrow, perilous trail that wound down the steep *tepui*. The descent was slow and tedious, and Vicard continually muttered under his breath and shook his head, his bravado replaced with worry. And for good reason. One wrong step, and a gust of wind might pitch him several hundred feet down the side of the *tepui*. On the other hand, the view of the verdant plain below was stunning; Indy couldn't wait to get there.

The further they descended, the less the wind howled and the easier it was to walk. But as they made their way around a massive boulder, an unseen portion of the *tepui* came into sight, and with it a new obstacle. A tremendous wall of water gushed over the top of the *tepui*. The stream Indy had seen at the pool must have merged with other streams and grown into a river before it spilled over the side.

"Oh, dear," Vicard said. "I'm not looking forward to this."

"How are we going to get past that?" Indy asked.

"Don't worry," Salandra said. "We don't have to jump into this one."

"That's nice to know."

"The path leads behind it," she explained. "Just be careful where you step."

"Thanks for the reminder. I have a bad habit of forgetting that."

When they reached the falls, Indy was awed by its raw power. Tons of water poured over the edge every second, and plunged hundreds of feet. Indy clamped his fedora down on his head as he stepped behind the curtain of water. He was instantly drenched from the spray. The rocks were slippery, and the water pounded down with a tremendous force just inches from his head. Indy moved slowly, his eyes adjusting to the dimmer light. The water had carved a shallow cavity out of the rock, and he thankfully stepped back from the downpour.

As he waited for Salandra and Vicard to catch up, he peered ahead, trying to gauge the distance to the other side. That was when he saw them. Nine or ten men were gathered together less than a dozen yards away, and they were watching him intently.

"We've got company!" Indy barked over the deluge as Vicard and Salandra joined him.

The men, who were armed with the now familiar crossbows, started to move toward them. There was no place to go but back, and if they turned away they'd get shot with darts and probably tumble into the falls. Vicard raised a hand and shouted, "Don't worry. They're with us. My guard."

"Why didn't somebody tell me," Indy grumbled. But the pounding water drowned out his voice.

He stepped aside as Vicard moved ahead. The king, using hand signals, conferred briefly with one of the men. If they were mere guards, they certainly weren't acting very subservient to their king. None of them bowed, knelt or acted like humble subjects. Then Vicard turned and motioned Indy and Salandra to follow. They slowly crept past the curtain of water and out into the open again. Carefully, they worked their way over the wet rocks near the falls.

"Everything all right, Father?" Salandra asked as Vicard paused.

"No sign of any Wayua," Vicard said. Indy took off his hat and shook the water from it. "I guess I needed a shower." But he'd strayed too close to the edge. The rocks beneath him were wet, and he lost his footing. He grabbed for a handhold as he slid downward, but the rocks pulled loose as soon as he touched them. He was about to be sucked into the watery void of the falls, when a hand grabbed his collar, and with surprising strength pulled him from the grasp of certain death.

"Watch your step," Vicard said casually, letting go of him.

"Are you all right, Indy?" Salandra asked, clutching his arm.

Indy nodded, but his heart was pounding. He gaped at the king. "Thanks. I'm indebted."

Vicard shook his head. "If I hadn't stopped you from falling, how would you save my kingdom?"

"I don't know if I can save your kingdom, sir, but I'll do whatever I can to get that staff away from Maleiwa. You can count on it."

"That's all I ask, my son," Vicard said. "The rest will follow."

As they moved away from the falls, Indy glimpsed the king's guard far ahead on the trail. They were moving rapidly, and were mere specks on a wavy line. "Why don't your men show you more respect?" Indy asked. "I didn't see any of them bow or salute you."

Vicard laughed. "Maybe that's the way people act toward kings in your world, but in Pincoya there is no need for any show of veneration. If anything, I should bow to them. Those men saved my life when the Wayua attacked my palace."

They plodded forward in silence, but Indy had decided that he liked Vicard. If kings in his world had been like Vicard, they might not be a virtually extinct species of ruler. Besides, there was something familiar and comfortable about him, something he couldn't quite figure out.

He wondered why Vicard had called him son. Certainly, he was old enough to be Indy's father, but . . . Then he recalled what Salandra had said about doubles. Maybe Vicard knew, or rather believed, as Salandra did, that she and Indy were sister and brother, of sorts.

If doubles actually existed, Indy wondered who would be Vicard's counterpart in his world. Vicard didn't remind him much of his stern father, and he was more like an American president than any king Indy could think of. He was warmer than the tight-fisted Calvin Coolidge, but not as brassy as Teddy Roosevelt. And what about Maleiwa? Who would he . . . As soon as the question formed, Indy knew the answer. If there were doubles, Maleiwa's was Hitler.

After another hour or so of walking, they were near

the base of the *tepui*. Vicard's guards awaited them at
a point where the trail split into two arms.

"We go this way," Salandra said, pointing toward
the grassy plain.

Indy suddenly felt uneasy. They'd be visible from
nearly a mile away. "Where's the other trail lead?"

"Through Swampland," Salandra said. "It's a more
direct route to Wayua, but far more difficult."

"Won't the Wayua be patrolling the plains, looking
for us?" Indy asked, as he gazed out toward the waving sea of grass.

"I doubt it," Vicard said in a confident tone. "The
last thing Maleiwa would think is that we would go
after him in his own territory. He probably thinks
we're hiding in fear in one of the Roraima caverns."

"Besides, the guard will be watching out for any
patrols," Salandra said in an encouraging voice as
they moved ahead on the trail leading toward the
grassland.

Indy didn't want to argue, but he was the one who
was supposed to get the alicorn, not Vicard or Salandra. "Maybe we should go the other way," he suggested. "It would provide a good cover as well as
being a shortcut."

"No," Vicard spoke in a firm, kingly voice. "You
don't understand. You would not make it out alive.
There are creatures in there you don't want to encounter."

"I suppose there would be a lot of snakes," Indy
conceded.

"Much worse," Salandra said. "Flying snakes."

"You know, I think you're right. Let's stay on this
route."

"Now what are they doing?" Vicard asked, peering

ahead. The guards had just made a quick about-face, and were racing across the grassland, motioning them to run.

"There's your answer," Indy barked. A couple of dozen men on horseback charged toward them across the open fields. He couldn't tell who they were, but it didn't take much to figure out that they were Wayua warriors.

They raced back toward the *tepui*, and had just reached the base of it where the trail split when the first of the horsemen reached them. He fired his crossbow and hit one of the guards in the neck. Indy hurled his whip, which curled around the warrior, and jerked him from his saddle. The warrior jumped up and aimed his crossbow at Indy, but was shot in the heart by one of the guards.

"Indy, run!" Salandra yelled.

Indy glanced at the approaching horsemen, and retrieved his whip. Most of Vicard's guards were staying behind to fight. One of them shoved Indy, and pointed. "Go!"

Indy hesitated a moment, then dashed after Vicard and Salandra along the trail toward swampland. They quickly entered a dank, humid slough. The ground was soggy where it was not covered with water, and he repeatedly sank in muck to his knees. Several warriors gave pursuit, but their horses were quickly bogged down. Two of the them pursued on foot, but Vicard's guards were waiting. The guards shot their pursuers with darts, and tossed their bodies into the watery muck where they quickly sank from sight.

When it was apparent they had escaped, Vicard ordered everyone to gather together, and he counted heads. The three of them and four of the guards had

survived, but Indy knew that Salandra was right
about the swamp. It was a horrid place, and their
chances of crossing it didn't look good. They moved
on.

Fingers of greenish fog rose from rancid pools of
water, and most of the trees were dead, and draped in
scaly, gray moss. The swamp smelled of decay, but
not the fresh smell of a living forest. It stank of
sulphur and the putrid odor of rotting flesh. A snake
that looked suspiciously like a fer-de-lance wriggled
across Indy's path and into a tangle of roots. A short
while later, Indy glimpsed another snake hanging
from the limb of a leafless tree. At least it didn't have
wings, he thought. He hoped Salandra had been exag-
gerating about the flying snakes.

"I'm glad it never gets dark here," Indy said. "It's
bad enough in the light." If darkness ever did fall,
they couldn't go anywhere without taking the chance
of being swallowed into a pool of water and muck.
"But where are we going to sleep?"

"We must keep going," Vicard said. "We cannot
sleep here. We would be easy prey."

Indy gazed up at a menacing vulture that eyed
them from a craggy limb. "I see what you mean." The
vulture suddenly took wing, as a horrific scream of
anguish cut through the swamp.

"What was that?" Salandra asked.

One of Vicard's guards raced toward them, waving
his hands and pointing toward the sky. Then he dove
headfirst into the swamp, and clutched the trunk of a
small tree.

"Get down!" Vicard barked, and Indy dropped
facedown into the muck. An earsplitting cry from
overhead sent an icy shiver down his spine. He was

paralyzed with fear, but he had to see what it was. He forced himself to raise his head.

The sky was filled with a black form, and at first Indy couldn't imagine what it was. Then he saw massive, leathery wings, and a prehistoric head that was all teeth and cold, dark eyes. The body of the creature was thick and snakelike, but it had a pair of legs equipped with huge claws. At first, Indy couldn't make out what the creature was carrying. Then he looked on in horror as he realized the claws gripped the limp body of one of the guards.

The creature let out another shrill, deafening cry, and Indy felt like burying himself in the muck. Then the beast was gone, and the swamp was silent. Slowly, he dug himself from the muck and helped Salandra to her feet. "Was that the flying snake?"

"Yes, a dragon," she answered. "And it's probably got a mate around here, too."

21

THINGS IN THE SWAMP

Indy had always wanted to see a dragon when he was a kid. But now that he'd seen one, he'd decided he didn't want to encounter another. They trudged on through the swamp in silence, the three remaining guards now staying close by them. They all peered warily toward the sky from time to time, but no dark shadow fell across them, and no shrill, piercing cry shattered the false tranquility.

The deeper they penetrated the swamp, the harder it became to find dry ground. Several times they ended up on muddy spits on land with water everywhere. Each time, they backtracked and tried another course, only to be trapped again. Finally, after retreating from yet another dead-end, they decided to stop and eat a quick meal while the guards searched for a way around the high water.

Indy settled on a tree stump that had been worn nearly flat and, Salandra handed him a bowl filled with beans and dried fruit. He'd no sooner popped several pieces of the fruit into his mouth when Salandra cried out.

His eyes darted skyward; he looked all around him. "What is it?"

"There's a hole in the side of that stump, and I just saw something poke its head out."

Indy leaped to his feet, nearly spilling the contents of the bowl. He kicked the stump, and a furry spider the size of his fist crawled out, then another, and another. He backed away shaking his head, and bumped into Salandra. "I think I'll eat standing up."

"You should sit somewhere," said Vicard, who was sitting on the pack that contained their food supply. "We've still got a good walk ahead of us yet, even if we find higher ground."

"How good?" Indy asked, as he spread out his leather jacket and sat down on it.

Vicard laughed. "Very good. But I'm sure we can make it out of here before we get too tired to walk. We've just got to find a way around the water."

This place was starting to sound like the maze, Indy thought, as he ate a handful of pea-shaped beans that tasted vaguely like peanuts. The dried fruit wasn't bad, either, sort of like a cross between pineapple and peach.

A faint cry caught his attention.

"Did you hear that?" Salandra asked.

"I think it was one of the guards," Vicard asserted. "You two wait here. I'm going to take a look."

"Father, please."

"I'll go," Indy said.

"No. You stay with Salandra. I won't be long."

"Don't go far, please," Salandra said, as Vicard walked away.

"He won't let his men down," she added with a sigh as Vicard disappeared from sight.

Indy was suddenly feeling tired again. He wondered how many hours or days they could walk before they couldn't take another step. When he considered that falling asleep would be the equivalent of conceding to death, he figured he could go at least three days without sleep as long as they had food and water. And *nalca.* Salandra surprised him by saying she thought they could go at least five days. The constant illumination of the interior world made it easier to stay awake longer, and most people slept no more than four hours a day.

"It seems like I sleep all the time here," Indy said as he finished eating.

"Only while you're adjusting to the change." Salandra frowned. "Indy, he's been gone a long time."

"I wouldn't worry about him, yet." It did seem as if Vicard had been away quite a while, but Indy no longer trusted his sense of time.

"No, he should be back by now." She took several steps in the direction that Vicard had gone. "Father! Father!" She called out again and again, but there was no answer. "We should've gone with him. He has a poor sense of direction."

"I'll go look for him."

"Not without me, you won't."

"All right." Indy stuffed his jacket into the pack and slung it over his shoulder.

"Let me carry it," she said.

"What, you don't trust me with the food?"

"It's not that. You may need your hands free."

He shrugged and handed it to her. "Let me know if it gets too heavy."

They headed off in the direction Vicard had gone. There was probably no reason for concern. But then again, why hadn't Vicard answered her calls? Indy shouted his name. His voice sounded hollow and eerie. He thought he heard a rumble in the distance, and was about to ask Salandra if she'd heard it, when he spotted the first body. It was one of the guards; his neck was broken.

"Oh, no!" Salandra gasped. "Father!"

"Shh! Don't say a word," Indy hissed. They moved on and found another guard. His heart had been ripped out. A short distance away Indy came upon the last guard. His body was badly mauled; it looked as if something had been eating him.

Salandra was holding her hands to her face, weeping softly. Indy led her away from the bodies, and at the same time looked around for Vicard's remains.

He spun around as he heard a grunting noise. He peered through the tall, barren trees, expecting to see the beast that had killed the men. Instead, he spotted Vicard standing near a cluster of dead trees. The king raised a hand and motioned Indy and Salandra away, but it was too late.

"Father!" Salandra sprinted toward him. "I was so worried about you." A huge man dressed in leather armor and covered with blood stepped out from behind the trees. A mane of wild, black hair fell over his shoulders, and one of his eyes bulged from his head. He took three swift steps, caught Salandra by the arm, and lifted her in the air. A scar sliced his face from his bad eye to his jaw, and his nose looked as if someone or something had chewed on it.

Indy hurled his whip at the giant. It wrapped around his neck, but the brute immediately snatched it and jerked Indy toward him. He dropped Salandra, grabbed the archaeologist by the back of his neck, and tossed him a dozen feet through the air.

The bloodthirsty brute was coming for Indy, his huge clawlike hands raised above his head. Indy backed away as fast as he could, but ran up against a tree. The giant was about to pounce on him, when he looked around. He bellowed angrily and turned in a circle.

At first, Indy didn't know what had distracted the giant. He started to crawl away, and realized that Salandra and Vicard were gone. A moment ago they'd been huddled in each other's arms a few feet away; now they'd vanished. Indy crawled a few more yards and his hand fell on his whip. He leaped to his feet and sprinted away, the whip trailing behind.

The giant bellowed savagely and rushed after him. Indy heard another rumble, but paid it no heed. He dodged between trees, sloshed through muck, tore through the bramble and vines. He tripped, glanced back, and saw the giant gaining on him. He scrambled to his feet, charged away, and waded right into a bog.

Muck rose to his knees, his thighs. He was stuck and sinking, and the more he struggled the faster he sank. The giant, more familiar with the surroundings, watched at the edge of the bog as the swamp swallowed Indy inch by inch.

It was either death by the swamp or death at the hands of the giant, Indy thought. He didn't want to get torn apart by the fiend, but he couldn't just let himself sink, either. The muck was sucking at his chest. He coiled his muddy whip, and hurled it with all of his might at the giant. It struck his leather vest, but dropped harmlessly at his feet.

Swell. Just swell. Indy hurriedly reeled in the whip, and made one last desperate attempt to snare the giant's legs as the bog rose under his armpits.

The brute reached out and grabbed the whip, but simply held it with both hands. Indy pulled; the giant pulled back, then dropped the whip. That was it. Indy was through. The muck was up to his chin, and the beastly giant was grinning like a maniac, apparently enjoying his victim's predicament.

Indy flailed his arms, frantically trying to stay above the surface. But his weight was too much. He leaned his head back, gulped his last breath of air, and squeezed his eyes shut as the bog swallowed his head. He clawed at the muck, and his hands broke the surface, but he couldn't get his head out of the water. As soon as he let out his air, it would all be over.

He felt a jerk on the whip, then a second, and a third. The giant wasn't trying to pull him out. He wanted the whip. Indy clung to it; if he died, the whip was going with him. He wrapped it several times around his forearm just as the last of his air escaped and his arms slipped under the surface.

The muck had claimed him as its own. It was almost over. His energy was exhausted; his life waned. He couldn't move. Dead at thirty, he thought. It didn't matter. Oddly, the moment that he'd accepted death, he was no longer frightened. He felt a warm glow around him. He was almost happy.

He vaguely felt another tug on his arm, and then his head popped through the muck. Abruptly, the warmth and happiness vanished, replaced with pain.

Indy sputtered, gasping for breath. He hurt all over. His body was one sentient pain. Then he realized the giant was dragging him out of the muck and into his vile grasp.

Indy vainly tried to untangle himself from the whip, but the giant was pulling too hard and too fast. He felt hot breath on his face as a massive hand squeezed his throat, let up, squeezed again. *He's playing with me.*

A high-pitched shriek rang in Indy's ear. He glanced up just in time to see another dragon swoop down. Its talons burrowed into the giant's hair, and the brute roared as he dropped Indy. His arms windmilled and he howled in pain as a talon slashed his forehead, then dug into his shoulder. The dragon's head darted toward the giant's throat, but caught his forearm instead in its snakelike jaws. Then, with a raucous screech, the dragon released the giant, and flew off.

Indy sucked in air, recovering his breath. He fumbled to untangle the whip, which was wrapped around his forearm and one leg. But he was too slow. The giant, reeling in circles, wiped blood from his eyes as he stumbled over Indy's prone body. Angrily, he slammed his heel into Indy's back, pressing him into the wet earth. He raised his foot, and was about to crush Indy's spine when the earth rumbled. It was much louder than the earlier rumblings. An earthquake, he thought.

Then a roar compounded the din as a two-legged reptilian monster stomped into view. It towered over them, making even the giant seem diminutive. A dinosaur! Indy saw a mouth filled with jagged teeth, each one the size of his hand or larger; heard the snap of its jaw just above the giant's head. The brute loped away, his wounded arm hanging limply at his side. But Indy cracked his whip, snagging the giant's ankle; it spun and charged Indy, intent on tearing him to pieces. But the dinosaur found his dinner first. He swatted the giant, knocked him off his feet, and crushed him in his gigantic jaws.

And I'm dessert, Indy thought, scrambling for the trees. The earth rumbled again. The man-eating monster was on his trail. He rushed ahead, but stopped when he saw the pack that Salandra had carried away from camp.

What the hell was it doing here? But when he spotted the remains of the giant a short distance away, he realized he'd run in a circle. As he snatched up the pack, a feather fluttered to the ground. Rumbling rocked the earth again, and he dashed away. But he didn't get far. There was water in front of him, water to his left, a bog on his right. Trapped! And the ground beneath his feet quaked.

A huge log lay near the water's edge. On second glance Indy realized it was a primitive dugout. He skidded down to the embankment, and found a roughly hewn paddle inside. He didn't know who owned it, but he was going to borrow it. He shoved as hard as he could, trying to free the craft from the shore. It would literally take a giant to pull it up so far, he thought. Then he knew whose dugout he was taking.

A roar from the beast gave Indy an extra surge of power. The dugout broke free and floated. He hopped inside, and slammed the paddle into the water. But the dinosaur plunged in after him. Two or three more strides and it would be all over. The creature would devour Indy and use the dugout for a toothpick.

A shrill wail erupted just yards behind him. The creature swatted at the water, and a huge wave washed over the side of the dugout. But Indy was picking up speed. He glanced back and saw the dinosaur sinking slowly into the slime. Its legs were stuck, and it could no longer move. It bellowed and bellowed.

"Tough luck, fellow," Indy muttered, as he paddled away as fast as he could go. "Believe me, I know just what it's like."

Indy slid through the swamp, winding past dead trees and over gnarled roots. The rumbles, bellows, and roars were replaced with silence and stillness. If he hadn't been so filthy and exhausted, he might actually have been enjoying himself. He was tempted to flop into the water and wash off the dried mud that was caked over his entire body, but he wasn't about to leave the dugout. Who knew what waited below the surface of these murky waters?

Indy was alone, lost, with no sense of direction. He tried to avoid going in circles, but everything looked the same. More than an hour, maybe two had passed when a bird, a falcon perhaps, flew overhead and screeched at him. He took it, at the very least, as a portent. He had nothing to lose. He turned in the direction the bird had flown.

Sometime later, Indy heard another screech, and saw a Great Horned Owl perched high on a limb of a barren tree, a loner standing in the water. Another favorable portent. Or so he hoped.

He paddled on. The dominant tree now was a banyanlike species with thick trunks that looked like vertical coils of rope. The lower branches spawned hanging roots, which burrowed into the water, forming secondary trunks. The farther Indy paddled in the watery forest, the greener the trees became. The branches of some of them sagged with elongated pods that looked like huge green sausages. As the landscape turned verdant, the atmosphere itself seemed to change. The sky was a pale green, and the foreboding feeling of the swamp vanished. Indy was exhausted, but he felt better than he had since they'd left the *tepui*.

He reached a channel that was bordered by what looked like mangroves. Green and alive. The water actually appeared to be clear now, and he saw small fish swimming about. He paddled down the channel, taking his time. It was warm, but not hot, and the green thicket eventually gave way to a white, sandy beach.

He jumped from the dugout, and for an instant wondered if he'd made a mistake. But the bottom was sandy and firm. He flopped down in the warm, shallow water, stripped off his muddy garments, bathed, then washed and wrung out his clothes. He laid them out on the beach to dry, and stretched out on the warm sand. In a moment, he was sound asleep.

22

JOURNEY TO WAYUA

In his dream, Indy saw a band of unicorns charging
down a green hill and crossing a lowland. They were
majestic creatures with shiny, white pelts that covered muscular limbs. Their heads were noble, and
their horns glistened in the pale green light. They
slowed, and their leader warily approached a water-
ing spot. There was someone here. Someone sleeping.

Then Indy saw that it was himself.

The unicorn appraised him, as the others slowly
approached. The leader lowered his head and pointed
its horn at Indy's heart, and pressed. The horn penetrated Indy's skin. It was piercing his heart. Indy
tried to tell himself to wake up before he was killed.
But then he realized it was just a dream.

To his amazement, he saw Salandra on the beach
among the unicorns. Her copper hair shone like
metal; and her features seemed softer. Her emerald
eyes glowed as if they were the center of her being.

She approached the leader and stroked its mane, and the beast withdrew its horn from Indy's chest. The unicorn raised its head high and led the others to the water's edge, where they drank deeply.

Salandra glided over the sand to where he was watching his dream. She leaned close to him, and whispered in his ear. "You and I are one. One."

"This is a dream," he answered.

She smiled, then turned her back to him. He embraced her from behind. She pressed her back to his chest, and sank into his flesh, his bones. They merged, and they were one.

A dream. Just a dream. But Indy felt a warmth and happiness that oddly reminded him of the moment in the muck when he had nearly died.

But it lasted only a moment. The feeling was replaced by a sense of alarm. He could no longer see. He was spinning. He felt as if he were shrinking. Then he changed; he was a falcon, soaring into the sky. The bird circled the water where the unicorns were still drinking, then it flew off over green hills which soon gave way to a brown, flat, scrub-covered desert.

A dream, Indy told himself again. But the fact that he knew it was a dream gave it a reality of its own. Everything below him seemed to vibrate and glow, as if the land itself were a living thing. The sky was now a pale brown that reflected the barren, sand-colored earth. Time and distance seemed to blur, as it always did in dreams.

The desert turned into a wide, sandy beach bordering a tranquil, pale green ocean. The falcon followed the coastline until an adobe city grew out of the arid land. Its narrow winding streets were crowded with people, many of them Wayua warriors with crossbows slung over their shoulders. The falcon skirted the city, then continued on.

Finally, the bird reached a rocky jut of land on which a massive castle was perched. The bird circled around it. At the center of the castle was an immense courtyard that was filled with colorful flags and a throng of people. The falcon swept low over the assembled crowd, then arced upward and landed on a rampart. The bird's vision was powerful, and it watched the proceedings with a certain human curiosity.

The men wore long tunics that covered their thighs. If they wore any pants, they were short. The women were even more peculiar looking. They were garbed in lightweight, brightly colored, billowy robes, but what was particularly striking was their two-tone faces. The left side, in every case, was painted black.

A procession of men on horseback carrying banners paraded through the center of the courtyard, and they were cheered on by the crowd. There was a medieval flavor to the proceedings, and the bird wouldn't have been surprised to see knights in full armor.

The bird suddenly swept low over the heads of the crowd, but all eyes were on the procession. The falcon landed near a wall, and a swirl of dust rose around it. Indy found himself crouched in an alcove. He stood up, and looked over his body as if seeing it for the first time. Salandra was poised nearby, peering out toward the procession.

"Where are we?"

"Maleiwa's fortress."

"We couldn't really be here," Indy murmured. "This is a dream."

Salandra's hypnotic eyes bored into him. "True enough. But we're here nevertheless."

They stepped out of the alcove, but Indy immediately jumped back as three men with crossbows strode toward him. They were each as large as the giant from the swamp. "Don't worry," Salandra said. "They can't see you."

"They were going to walk right into me."

"No. Right through you. Look, there he is!"

At the end of the procession, a muscular, bald man with strong features and sharp, dark eyes held his head high as he rode by on a white stallion. Indy recognized Maleiwa from the time in the tower in Pincoya. But there was something noticeably different about him now. He was stronger, more powerful in appearance. A force surrounded him, cloaked him in a shield of invincibility. In his right hand he held a staff and Indy's gaze fell on the crest, a silver, double-headed eagle.

The alicorn.

Indy couldn't take his eyes off the staff as Maleiwa raised it high above his head. The throng chanted. At first, he couldn't understand. They were speaking in a language he didn't know. But then the words surrounded him, pressed against him, and he was certain he was about to decipher the chant when Salandra whispered in his ear. "The Unicorn's Gate . . . The Unicorn's Gate. That's what they are saying."

Indy took a step toward Maleiwa as if drawn by the alicorn, but Salandra touched his arm. "Wait. You can do nothing now."

"What's going on? What's he doing?"

"Don't you know? He's on his way with the alicorn to your world."

Indy knew with a certainty that everything that Salandra had said about the Wayua leader was correct. He had to stop him.

He heard a distracting noise, a scratching sound that seemed to emanate from another place.

"I'm glad you finally see things as they are," Salandra said, as if reading his mind.

"Where is the Unicorn's Gate?" Indy asked, ignoring the scratching.

"It's less than a day's walk from where you are sleeping."

"Sleeping . . . where am I sleeping?" Although he'd been intent on convincing himself that he was dreaming, the thought that he was sleeping astonished him. Everything around him turned blurry, then faded, and the last thing he heard was the scratching noise.

Indy sat up, brushed off the sand, and then grabbed his clothes. They were bone dry, even on the underside. He quickly pulled them on. He must have slept at least a couple of hours.

A scratching sound. It was coming from a nearby patch of mangroves. He walked over and peered through the shrubs and saw the pack. How'd it get over there? He was sure he'd left it in the dugout. He glanced back over his shoulder. The dugout was gone.

More scratching. The pack moved. He heard a snuffling sound as if the thing were alive: He kicked it over. Beans and dried fruit spilled out, and a yellow liquid. A hole had been chewed into Salandra's skin pouch, and the *nalca* was seeping into the sand. He snatched up the pouch just as the last drops oozed out. He threw it down in disgust. No more *nalca*. Great. If he wasn't in trouble before, he was now.

His fedora inched out of the pack and crawled several feet across the sand. He took a couple of steps toward it as it edged further away. He reached down, but suddenly it skidded away and out of his grasp. "Hey! Come back here."

Indy chased after the hat, snatched it up, and a foot-long rodent ran off. He examined the inside of the hat, brushed it off, and placed it firmly on his head. He walked back to the pack and recovered what he could of the food.

"Rats."

Indy heard a splashing sound, and glimpsed the dugout gliding through the water. He couldn't see who was inside of it. He ducked down in the mangroves as the dugout eased up to the beach. Another giant? But then why was he still alive?

"Indy?"

"Salandra!" He stepped out of the mangroves as she and Vicard climbed out of the dugout and waded to shore. "You're alive!"

"Of course we are," she said. "We arrived yesterday while you were sleeping."

"Yesterday?"

"You slept at least fourteen hours," Vicard said.

"Why didn't you wake me?"

"You needed the sleep after those three days in Swampland," Vicard said. "We slept, too. We took turns, of course."

Three days. It seemed impossible. He momentarily wondered if the time expansion he experienced here was related to the place, or something that Salandra and Vicard somehow effected. But he had more immediate questions on his mind. "How did you two get away from that giant so easily, and how did you find me here?"

"You already know the answers to those questions, Indy," Vicard said. "Now we must leave right away. There's no time to waste."

"I don't think I do know the answers. And where are we going?"

"Think about your dream. It's all there."

"What dream?" But the moment he asked, a flash of a dream came back to him. He was soaring over a desert, and then there was something about a castle and strange men on horses and women with one side of their faces painted black. Something important was going on, but he couldn't recall what it was.

Salandra peered curiously at him. "Do you remember now?"

He shrugged. "Sort of."

"It'll come back," she assured him.

They saved what they could of their supplies, and Vicard slung the pack with the remains of their food over his shoulder. "Ready, Indy?" he asked. "Hat, whip, jacket. You look ready." He laughed and slapped Indy on the middle of his back.

For a moment, Indy was annoyed by how hard Vicard had struck him. Then suddenly his dream came back to him with clarity and detail. "We can't go to Wayua," he said firmly. "Maleiwa isn't there anymore. He left." He glanced over at Salandra. "You were there. I mean in my dream."

Salandra and Vicard were silent, and he felt more and more confused as he related what he remembered, and tried to make sense of it. "But I guess it was just a dream, so it doesn't really matter." His voice trailed off.

"Of course it matters, Indy," Salandra said. "I'm pleased that you've remembered so much. We have to get to the Unicorn's Gate before he does. That's where we're headed."

She acted as if the entire thing had been real. He laughed nervously. "Then why don't we just fly there and save our feet?"

"You are very limited in what you can do when you and I are together in the bird-form. You have to get the alicorn away from Maleiwa on your own. As much as you would like, you cannot simply dream away your problems."

Look who's talking, he thought. "Why's it called the Unicorn's Gate?"

"Because at one time unicorns passed freely between worlds," Salandra said. "But their horns became so prized in your world that they retreated to the interior and guarded their gate. It became part of their survival instinct."

"A nice myth," Indy said as they set out.

"A true one, too," Vicard added.

They walked away from the beach and into a pleasant moorland. But when Indy stared toward the horizon, he felt disoriented. He quickly turned his gaze to the field in front of him, and away from the rolling, purple hills that rose in the distance and curved into the sky. If he stared too long at the horizon, he'd probably fall over.

"Are we in Wayua territory yet?" Indy asked a while later.

"We've been in it ever since we entered Swampland," Vicard said.

"I'm surprised anyone would claim that horrible place as their own," Indy commented.

"The Wayua put it to use," Salandra said.

"It's the place where the worst criminals are sent," the bearded king added. "We encountered one of them."

"The giant?"

"That's right."

"Many people in Wayua are as large as that man," Salandra commented. "His size is not unusual, but his crimes probably were."

"So the swamp is like a prison," Indy said.

"There's only one worse penalty."

"Death?" Indy asked.

"The swamp *is* death. But an even worse fate is to be sent through a gate and deprived of *nalca*," Vicard said.

A one-way ticket to the land of the lost, the maze, Indy thought, recalling what Salandra had told him. He wondered if it was true, but his thoughts turned back to the giant. He asked Vicard why the brute had spared him.

"He was planning to save me," the king answered. "He liked fresh meat, and he was full from feasting on one of the guards."

"A cannibal," Indy said in disgust. "I guess we're lucky we didn't run into more of them."

"They don't survive long in the swamp," Vicard explained. "There is precious little to eat, except each other, but the prisoners are usually quickly disposed of by the beasts."

"It's a harsh penalty."

"And usually a fitting punishment, for most of

them." After a moment, Vicard added: "I only wish Maleiwa would end up there himself."

"No. He deserves the maze, and he'll get it." Salandra's voice was hard, unforgiving. "He's already responsible for hundreds of deaths, and if he is allowed to continue, the dead will be stacked high in both worlds."

The last two words—*both worlds*—rang in Indy's head. In spite of all he'd seen and experienced, he couldn't say for certain that he was actually inside the earth. It clearly seemed that he was, yet . . .

"You still don't believe what you see, do you?" Salandra said. "After all your experiences."

Indy laughed self-consciously, wondering how she'd guessed at his thoughts. "It defies everything that I know about what is real," he said as they plodded along. "But right now I'm just glad the ground underneath my feet is solid, and I'll be glad when we're closer to the hills, so I don't have to see the distant ones climbing sideways up the sky. I'm not looking any further than that."

23

THE UNICORN'S GATE

By the time they had crossed the moorlands and entered the hills, a thick fog hugged the ground. It didn't matter whether they were walking through a valley or over a crest. The fog never rose higher than Indy's waist, and the way it folded over the hills made it seem as if they were walking through a bed of clouds.

The reality of the situation was another matter. They stumbled from time to time as they stepped on invisible rocks, and Indy was constantly wary of walking off an unseen cliff. The best thing that could be said about the fog, as far as Indy was concerned, was that their view of the horizon from the hilltops resembled a cloudy day, rather than the crazy, concave distortion that would never be either welcome or familiar to him.

The fog gave the landscape a dreamy appearance.

Indy could easily imagine the unicorns he'd seen in his dream galloping through it.

"How much longer before we reach the gate?" he asked after they'd mounted the fourth or fifth hill.

"It's not that kind of gate," Salandra said. "It's very difficult to locate, because it drifts."

Swell. Indy knew about revolving doors, but drifting gates guarded by unicorns were something else altogether. "Then how are we going to find it?"

"We'll leave that to Maleiwa. He can find the gate with the alicorn. That's been his plan all along."

"Where does it lead?"

"No one knows for certain. It's shifted over the years with changes in your world and ours. It could lead right to Germany, as I'm sure Maleiwa hopes, or to Trafalgar Square, but it could also drop you in the Arctic."

"What?"

"Sorry."

"I should've brought a scarf."

So they didn't know where to find the gate, or where it would take them. They were in real good shape, Indy thought. "But why would Maleiwa take a chance on ending up in some impossible place? I don't get it."

"His arrogance is getting the better of him," Vicard said. "He thinks that, with the help of the alicorn, he can actually manipulate where the gate will open."

"Can he?" Indy asked.

Vicard shrugged. "I don't know."

"Swell. What else don't you know?"

"Where to find Maleiwa," Vicard said.

"You're kidding, aren't you?" Indy could tell that he wasn't.

They stopped as they reached another hilltop. Wisps of fog threaded around Vicard's waist; with his red beard and robust appearance, he looked like a mythical god rising from the sea. "It's up to you, Indy. Tell us which way to go."

"How would I know? I thought you two knew where we were going."

Vicard tapped a finger to his chin as he considered Indy's comment. "Only to a point, and we've reached it. I'm actually not very good at directions."

Indy glared at Vicard. At the moment, he didn't look so much like a mythical god as a bumbling old man.

"Concentrate on the alicorn," Salandra said. "It was once in your possession. You should be able to sense its location."

Indy wasn't at all sure of that. Nevertheless, he looked out toward the next hill, which resembled a soft, fluffy cloud. He turned left, then right. He shrugged. "I guess I don't sense alicorns very well."

"Come, Indy," Salandra urged. "You've got to try harder. Sit down."

"Here, in this soup?" Indy reached down and felt grass, then sank into the fog.

Salandra was to his right, Vicard to his left. "Look into the fog," she said. "Picture Maleiwa carrying the alicorn. Where is he now?"

Indy stared intently ahead. At first, nothing happened. No matter how hard he tried to imagine Maleiwa carrying the alicorn, he couldn't see him. Even the images from his dream had nearly faded. He could only vaguely imagine Maleiwa parading across a courtyard.

"You're trying too hard," Salandra whispered. "Relax."

How could he relax when he was being asked to do the impossible? *Forget it,* Indy thought.

The moment he stopped trying to see Maleiwa, the fog seemed to grow more dense. It seeped right through him, and then he saw Maleiwa riding a horse up a hill. He was wearing long pants and a jacket, dressed like a man of the exterior world. Three other men were with him, and fog covered all of them to the haunches of the horses. But protruding from the fog was the silver crest of the alicorn.

Indy stared intently at the silver, double-headed eagle. Of course. The eagle was Indy's guardian bird, it had been for years, and it had guided him through hard times on several occasions. It could work for him now, if he called upon it.

"Which way?" he asked. He didn't know whether he'd spoken the words under his breath or aloud. He didn't care. He stood up, and for a moment glimpsed a majestic bald eagle soaring over the hill to his right. He pointed toward the bird, but it was gone.

"That way?" Salandra asked.

"Yeah. That way," Indy answered, not bothering to say anything about the eagle. It was his bird, and there was no reason to say any more.

Neither Vicard nor Salandra questioned Indy's choice. The three of them moved off through the low fog, descending the hill and ascending the next one. Indy had not even considered what they would do when they found the Wayua leader. He'd face that matter when the time came. They paused at the top of the hill, saw no sign of Maleiwa or his men, then moved on, proceeding in the same general direction.

Maybe he was mistaken about the direction. What if there was no significance to the eagle he'd seen? For all Indy knew, they were heading the wrong way. Maybe they'd never find Maleiwa. But on the next rise, he forgot all about his concern. It was just as he'd seen it: Maleiwa and three of his men were approaching a hill on horseback, except now Maleiwa was gripping the alicorn by the shaft just below the crest, and holding it out in front of him.

Indy's eyes focused on the silver eagle heads; he was mesmerized by the sight. Then Vicard dropped to one knee and pulled Indy and Salandra down into the fog with him. They watched in silence as Maleiwa dismounted, and climbed the hill on his own while his men waited.

Indy crept forward, staying below the fog. Vicard and Salandra followed. Every so often Indy poked his head through the fog. Finally, he stopped a hundred feet short of the guards, and watched. Maleiwa held the alicorn by the crest with both hands, and slowly turned in a circle. He looked as if he were witching for water, but Indy knew better.

Indy ducked down, and crept ahead. He felt his way carefully, making sure not to loosen a stone or make any noises. He knew the guards were close by.

"Indy!" Salandra called out from behind him.

Great. Let's have a conversation. He raised his head and saw that the fog was dissipating, and the guards had spotted them.

"Run!" Vicard shouted.

But it was too late. The guards rushed toward them, crossbows drawn. They were surrounded. Trapped. Indy slowly raised his hands, and glanced toward the top of the hill. The only fog that remained formed a tunnel a few feet in front of Maleiwa and it led straight out from the hillside. Maleiwa had paused a step from the entrance. He turned to them, and grinned. "Too bad, Vicard. Your daughter and her counterpart are too late. Shoot them with death darts."

Indy belatedly reached for his whip. As the guards fired, Vicard dived in front of Indy. Three darts struck him in the chest and shoulder. Salandra screamed, and clutched her father. The guards raised their weapons to fire again.

But at that moment, one of the guards shouted and pointed toward the base of the hill. A herd of horses was charging toward them. No, unicorns!

The same ones from his dream, Indy thought in amazement. They charged up the hill, their heads down. The guards fired wildly, then scattered as the unicorns rushed at them. But the beasts were too fast. One of the guards tripped and he was instantly trampled. Another one held up his hands as if to appease the unicorns. A moment later, he was impaled and tossed through the air. The third guard disappeared over the hill, but his screams a moment later told of his fate.

"The gate!" Salandra shouted. "Go, Indy! Go!"

Maleiwa was gone, and the tunnel of fog was fading. Indy started for it, then turned back to Salandra, who held her father's head in her lap. "Are you coming?"

She laid her father gently down, and stood up. "I can't, Indy. I have to help Father."

"You mean he's alive?"

"I can bring him back. There's still time. Now go!"

He hugged her, and she whispered something in his ear.

"I'll remember that," Indy said. He hesitated a moment longer, then saw a majestic white unicorn rushing his way. It lowered its head, and at first Indy thought it was attacking him. Then he recognized it as the leader, the one that had pierced his heart in the dream.

As Indy dashed toward the gate, the unicorn moved alongside of him, and he grabbed its mane and leaped onto its back. The beast charged up the hill, but now Indy could see only a trace of the tunnel. He was sure that the unicorn was going to charge right through it, but suddenly it stopped, and Indy was catapulted through the air.

He tumbled head over heels and raised his arms over his head, expecting to strike the hillside. But he kept going . . . and going. He soared through the fog, which was not only visible, but was swirling around him. Then he was enveloped in a bright cloud, and he squeezed his eyes shut. He had no sense of speed or direction; he didn't know whether he was falling or climbing. Then he struck something solid.

Slowly, he raised his head. He lay on a dome-shaped, metallic surface that was tinged with green. Maybe copper. The surface was uneven, but he managed to stand up. At first, all he could see was pale blue sky, and below it a darker blue mixed with spots of churning white. Whitecaps. An ocean. He was perched about a hundred yards above it on a tiny copper island. But what was it? Where was he?

He noticed long spikes protruding from the edges. He turned and saw several things at once. He glimpsed a huge torch held by a massive hand, and he saw a skyline of tall buildings. New York! He was standing on the crown of the Statue of Liberty.

But before he could comprehend any of it, he spotted Maleiwa near the edge of the head. He was peering over the side, and he held the alicorn in his right hand. Indy loosened his whip and crept toward him. Maleiwa moved a few feet to one side and continued looking over the side. He was probably searching for a way down. Indy didn't know what they were doing on top of the Statue of Liberty, but it was a fitting spot to end the threat from Maleiwa once and for all.

Catch him off guard. Snag the alicorn with his whip and jerk it out of Maleiwa's grasp. That was his plan. Simple. Nothing to it. Beyond that, everything was up in the air, so to speak. Indy didn't know how long Maleiwa could last without the alicorn or *nalca*. But he'd find out. He calculated the distance to the alicorn, and pulled his arm back. What if he missed? His momentary hesitation cost him. Maleiwa spun around, gripped the alicorn in both hands, and held it over his head like a samurai warrior.

Face to face with Maleiwa for the first time, Indy realized the bald man was nearly as large as the giant from the swamp. He stood at least seven feet tall, and probably weighed nearly three hundred pounds. Indy was no match for him. Maleiwa would toss him over the side without a second thought. Indy hurled the whip, but Maleiwa instantly swung the alicorn downward in a circular path to his right, and the whip tumbled harmlessly over Maleiwa's left shoulder.

"Now I've got my hands full," Indy said under his breath.

Maleiwa pointed the alicorn at him. Indy prepared

to dodge the Wayua's attack, but Maleiwa was still recovering from his surprise.

"Good going, Jones," Maleiwa said, as Indy quickly reeled in his whip. "You've made it back to your world. Now you can die here." He lunged at Indy with the alicorn, but missed him by inches. Maleiwa quickly recovered, and pointed the alicorn at Indy again. "Consider yourself lucky. You get to live a few seconds longer."

"Just give up, Maleiwa," Indy said. "Give me the alicorn and go back and never return."

Maleiwa laughed. "You're a fool, Jones. There is no going back, not through this entrance. It's gone. Besides, I have business to attend to in Germany."

"Then you've got a problem, because I'm not going to let you walk away with the alicorn," Indy said. He noticed a pouch tied around Maleiwa's waist, and realized that the Wayua hadn't taken any chances. "I see you don't trust the power of the alicorn. You've brought along *nalca*."

"You're wrong. I know the alicorn's power, and it is protecting me. The *nalca* is for my ally, Herr Hitler. His scientists are going to reproduce it, so we will have a ready supply available for my army. Then the alicorn will be all Hitler's. At least for a while."

"I don't think Hitler has any scientists on his side. Like I told Salandra, he's a two-bit rabble-rouser."

"Don't count on it, Jones." Maleiwa swung the alicorn, but Indy ducked just in time. Maleiwa reversed directions, swinging the staff across his shoulder at Indy's head, but Indy blocked the blow with the coiled whip. Maleiwa pulled back on the relic, but Indy hung firmly onto it.

Anyone looking up at the Statue of Liberty at that

moment would've seen two men turning in an awk-
ward dance on the head of the majestic statue. But
the ballet didn't last long. Maleiwa forced Indy toward the edge, and Indy knew his only hope was to
hang onto the alicorn.

Indy's back slammed against one of the upright
spikes on the crown. He groaned, but refused to let
go of the staff. He jerked up his legs and shoved with
all of his strength against Maleiwa's chest. He caught
the Wayua off guard and pulled the alicorn away from
him. Maleiwa was enraged. He rammed into Indy,
and lunged for the relic.

Indy was so intent on hanging onto the staff that he
forgot his precarious position. The impact knocked
him from the spike. He hung for a moment, one hand
on the rim of the crown. The observation deck on the
lower part of the crown was right in front of him, and
several people gaped at him. All he had to do was
swing forward and grab one of the braces with his
legs.

But he lost his grip and slid down over the statue's
hairline, over the forehead, and onto the bridge of the
nose. Desperately, he dug his heels into the metal
and came to a stop at the end of the nose. His feet
dangled in midair, but somehow he still held onto the
alicorn.

Indy looked down—a mistake. He inched his way
back up until his feet were pressed against the nose.

"Jones, climb up a little and throw me the whip,"
Maleiwa yelled, as he leaned over the side of the
crown. "I'll pull you up."

"No thanks, pal."

Indy heard voices from the observation deck.
"Look at him down there!"

"All part of the show," he said under his breath.

"Someone's coming after him," a voice shouted.

Indy looked up and saw Maleiwa lowering a leg over the edge of the crown. "Where does he think he's going?" Indy lifted the alicorn over his head, gripping it below the crest. "Maleiwa, you want it? Then go get it!" With that, he hurled the alicorn toward New York Harbor. It flipped end over end, and shattered against the tablet held by Liberty. The double-headed eagle crest slid over the engraved date of the Declaration of Independence, and for a moment looked as if it were going to get caught in the fingers of Liberty. Then it fell away.

"No! No!" Maleiwa shouted, still clinging to the rim of the crown. He pulled himself back up to the top, but with great effort. He was losing his strength already, Indy thought. Now he was fumbling with the *nalca* pouch.

Indy climbed to the bridge of the nose, then hurled the whip upward, snagging one of the braces in the lower part of the crown. Free of the alicorn, he quickly mounted the forehead and climbed over the hair of the statue. He grabbed the brace and was tempted to drop inside to the observation deck. But he wanted to make sure that Maleiwa didn't get away. He gripped the handle of the whip in his teeth, reached toward the upper edge of the crown, pulled himself up, and vaulted onto the dome again. Maleiwa was on the opposite side, leaning against a spike where he was lifting the pouch of *nalca* to his mouth with shaking hands.

With a smooth flip of his wrist, Indy cast his whip at Maleiwa. The end of the whip snapped against the Wayua's hand. The pouch flew from his grasp, *nalca* spilling out of it. Maleiwa scrambled across the dome, fell, and crawled toward the pouch. Frantically, he lunged for the *nalca*, but Indy kicked the pouch out of his reach. It slid between two spikes and over the back of the statue's head.

Maleiwa staggered toward the edge, groaning. Then he turned on Indy, and rushed at him with arms outspread, a lunatic in a rage. Indy wasn't expecting Maleiwa's burst of energy. He took a step backwards and slipped on a patch of spilt *nalca*.

Maleiwa dived at him. He flew over Indy's head and kept right on going, over the side. Indy turned and thought he saw the image of Maleiwa hovering in midair. He could see right through him. Then the Wayua disintegrated, vanished, and Indy swore he heard the sound of a bellowing beast and a horrified scream. Lacking *nalca* or the alicorn for protection, Maleiwa had been claimed by the maze.

Epilogue

"Marcus, we're living in a dream world if we ignore the existence of this inner earth. The world is hollow. I've been there. I know what's down there. Well, sort of. It's important for science, for our future, for our security, that we make contact with the interior world. They're ready for relations with us, at least on a limited scale."

Several days had passed since Indy had descended the Statue of Liberty, and he was meeting with Marcus Brody for the second time. Indy was anxious to spill the story to the press, to go to Washington and, if necessary, tell President Coolidge himself. Although he'd tried to deny the existence of the inner world while he was there, his confrontation with Maleiwa had been the breaking point. After he'd survived, he'd realized that Salandra had been telling him the truth. Another land, another people, existed within the earth.

He paced around Brody's office. The museum director sat back in his chair and watched him, as if he were scrutinizing a terra-cotta horse from the T'ang Dynasty to see if it was one of the many forgeries on the market.

Brody threaded and unthreaded his fingers as he listened. A slight furrow knitted his brow, but he made no attempt to interrupt.

"Of course I'm not the first person to discover the interior world. Many people from this side have been there and returned. But nobody believed them." Indy stopped in front of Brody's desk. On it was the letter he'd written Brody from Santa Marta. It was held in place by the silver double-headed eagle, all that remained of the alicorn. Indy had recovered it at the base of the statue. "You believe me, don't you, Marcus?"

"Well, it is true that many of the legends of primitive peoples speak of an underworld. Even the stories of hell might be founded in the interior world. It certainly sounds as if you experienced a sort of hell. However . . ." Brody leaned forward, placed his hands on the arms of his chair, and rose with an effort, as if he weighed several hundred pounds. He walked over to a map of the world on the wall.

"However, what?" Indy asked suspiciously.

"Let's look at another possibility about what happened to you, Indy."

Indy threw up his hands, exasperated. If Brody wouldn't believe him, no one would. "All right. Go ahead. Tell me I'm nuts."

"Not nuts. I just think you may have been the victim of an intricate illusion." Brody traced his finger along the western coast of South America and stopped near the bottom. "The region here on the border of Chile and Argentina is a land of lakes and islands, just as you described after you were taken aboard the so-called ghost ship."

"Marcus," Indy interrupted. "There are lots of places in the world with lakes and islands. But I told you this wasn't like anything else. You can't imagine the things you see there."

"Indy, please, just let me go on." Brody tapped the map. "This lakes region has baffled explorers for centuries. They've gotten lost and very confused and seen things that weren't there. It's a perfect place for pirates or a strange band of believers to live."

"Believers?"

"Yes. Believers in a hollow world. I say that Salandra was born into a cult of sorts, which believes that the earth is hollow and that they were living in it. Everything in her life seems to reflect what appears to be an interior world, and you were caught up in it. There was probably some division in the cult, and that's what the controversy was about."

"Marcus, that doesn't explain half of what happened to me."

"I'm just getting started, Indy. Will you listen?"

"I think I've heard enough. I'm going to talk to a reporter at the *Post*. He'll listen to me."

"Indy, for your own sake, listen to what I've got to say before you go to the press with this wild story." Marcus Brody motioned emphatically with his hands as he spoke. "They'll have a field day. You'll be the laughingstock of the city. You'll be driven from your teaching job."

Indy slumped down into a chair. "Go ahead. I'm all ears."

"Thank you. As I was saying, I think you were sub-jected to a hollow-earth cult that exists in South America. One faction of it is fascinated with what's going on in Germany right now, and wants to lure the Nazis into their web."

"What about the rest of it—the maze, the *tepuis* with the cities inside, that swamp with those crea-tures, the castle?" Indy protested.

"Okay. You were taken to a place near San Agustin, Colombia. We know that much. This underground travel and the maze are a bit puzzling, but I'll get to that in a minute. We do know that you then traveled by train to Santa Marta and you encountered the Kogi Indians. After that you were supposedly in the inte-rior world again. But I don't think so."

"How can you say that?" Indy snapped.

Brody held up a hand. "Please. Just listen. You were drugged, remember? I think a lot of things got jumbled. For instance, *nalca* happens to be the name of a prickly plant that grows in southern Chile, specif-ically on Chiloé. And Pincoya is not a city. It's the name of a mythical creature on Chiloé, a type of mer-maid with legs and no flippers."

"But I saw the fish," Indy interrupted. "They defi-nitely were interested in its eggs."

"I'm not saying you didn't see it. I'm just saying that many things you perceived were an illusion." Brody pointed to the map of South America again. "I think you were drugged on that mountain outside of Santa Marta, and taken to the Gran Sabana region of Venezuela. All this traveling could account for your loss of time. You were heavily drugged for long peri-ods."

"The Gran Sabana?" The name was vaguely famil-

iar to Indy. "Wait a minute. You mean the place Ar-
thur Conan Doyle wrote about in *The Lost World*,
with the dinosaurs living on the plateaus?"

Brody smiled and nodded as he opened a file folder
and spread out several photographs. "Take a look."
The photos showed mysterious, flat-topped mountains with sheer drops of thousands of feet, and numerous sensational waterfalls.

"It does look like the place," Indy conceded. "But
so what? That doesn't mean there's no interior world.
And it could have a similar-looking region. In fact,
Salandra said that the interior world is a reflection of
the outer world. They're counterparts."

Brody shuffled through the photos, then held one
of them out to Indy. "This mountain is the highest
one in the Gran Sabana. It's over nine thousand feet.
The name of it is Roraima."

Indy shrugged, but now he wasn't so certain. "Another counterpart, I guess."

"And the Indian name for those mesas is *tepui*. You
see? Think about it. Did you actually see any cities
inside them?"

"No, but—"

"Ideas were placed in your head, and the drug did
the rest, or most of it. You battled a giant and a dinosaur because that's what they wanted you to see. It
was probably something else altogether. And your
castle. That *was* a dream, wasn't it?"

"Yeah. Go on." Indy's confidence was waning.

"You probably spent some time in the border region of Venezuela and Colombia." Brody tapped the
map again. "It's called the Guajira peninsula." He
walked back to his desk, and opened an oversized
book to a marked page. "Take a look." It was a photo-

graph of a woman wearing a long, billowy gown. One side of her face was painted black.

"That's one of the Wayua women," Indy said, excitedly.

"No, a Guajira Indian. And Maleiwa is the name of a figure from Guajira mythology." Brody laid the book down, picked up another, and opened it. "Can you read this?"

Indy stared at a page of Rongo-rongo script. He shook his head. "Not anymore, Marcus."

"As I thought. It's too bad. I wrote Davina about your disappearance, and I just received a letter from her." He picked up an envelope from the desk, pulled out a sheet of paper, and handed it to Indy. Davina expressed her regrets at Indy's disappearance, then added: "Regarding any unknown sacred tablets, they don't exist, and even if they did, it would be best for them to remain hidden forever."

Indy walked over to the window and stared out toward Central Park. *The park is real,* he thought. *New York is real. I am real.*

Brody cleared his throat. "Don't get me wrong, Indy. I think more than a drug was involved. I would classify your experiences as shamanistic encounters. There are people, as you know, who believe strongly that they can manipulate what we consider normal reality. I think when a number of them focus on someone with a strong intent, they may actually be able to alter that person's awareness, too."

"That would be hard to prove, Marcus."

Brody held up his hand. "I didn't say it was scientific fact, and to tell you the truth, I'm not interested in proving it. But I do think this hypothesis is better than believing that you were in an interior world."

"I still find it hard to believe, Marcus. If there's no interior world, what was the point?"

"It obviously had something to do with your involvement with that ivory staff. This Maleiwa had probably followed you to the Anasazi ruins where you hid it. After you left, he dug it up. Then the two factions started fighting over it, and both of them believed that you had some sort of power because you had possessed it for a while."

Indy laughed. "You've got an explanation for everything, Marcus. But how did I get on top of the Statue of Liberty? Tell me that?"

"How did you get down?"

"I climbed down to the observation deck," Indy said.

"Then that's how you got up there. You climbed up. You just don't remember that part."

"Yeah, I only remember the unicorns."

Indy stopped by the window again, and glimpsed a young woman walking along the sidewalk across the street from the museum. He leaned closer. She was tall, with copper-colored hair, and walked with a graceful, easy step. Salandra!

Brody continued talking, unaware of Indy's sudden interest in the woman. "The only thing that bothers me is that I swear I saw that ship, the *Caleuche*, sink into the sea. They'd taken you, and I thought you were dead. That's hard to explain."

No, it couldn't be her, Indy thought. But maybe . . . She turned into the park, and he had an urge to dash out of Brody's office, down the stairs, out the door, and across the street. Then he saw a bearded man approach her, and take her arm. He couldn't see his face very well, but it looked like Vicard.

"I guess I fell captive to the *Caleuche* myth myself, as did Hans Beitelheimer. It haunts that island. And this matter with doubles is fascinating, too," Brody continued. "I don't know what to think of that."

He moved over the window and peered out over Indy's shoulder. "What are you looking at so intently?"

Indy took his eyes off the pair for a moment, and when he looked again, they were gone. Maybe it had been them, maybe not. "Our doubles, Marcus."

"*Our* doubles?"

"That's right. Now I know who Vicard reminded me of. You!"

Brody tapped his chin in a gesture that was exactly as Vicard had done it. "Well, it would be nice to be a king, I suppose."

They both laughed. Indy wasn't sure what to believe about what had happened to him. Calling it all a drug-induced illusion seemed like a convenient way of explaining away everything. But he still had a lot of unanswered questions. For instance, what had happened to Maleiwa?

But then Indy recalled Salandra's final words, and now they made sense to him. "When you go back, things will seem confused," she'd said. "You will question what is, and what is not. But just remember our saying here: 'The unity of all is all that is.' "

ABOUT THE AUTHOR

ROB MACGREGOR wrote *Indiana Jones And The Last Crusade*, a novel based on the movie script. He is also the author of *The Crystal Skull*, a novel of adventure and intrigue, and *The Rainbow Oracle* (with Tony Grosso), a book of color divination. His travel articles have appeared in the *Miami Herald, Los Angeles Times, Boston Globe, Newsday* and elsewhere. He is also a contributor to *OMNI* Magazine's "Anti-Matter" section. Besides his work as a writer, he has organized adventure tours to South America for travel writers, and led the first group of U.S. journalists to the Lost City in the Sierra Nevada of Santa Marta Mountains in Colombia in 1987. He lives in Boynton Beach, Florida, where he is at work on his next novel.